"I'm getting warm," she lied, motioning toward the fire. **"And it's been a long day. I am thinking I'm going to go lie down for a bit."**

"Do you mind if I follow you that way?"

Her cheeks warmed, and she thumbed through the number of ways she wanted to answer that question. *Yes, but only if we zip our bags together and you make love to me all night. Or, do you really think you sleeping next to me is a good idea?*

Instead, she went with the simple. "We all have to sleep somewhere."

He stared at her, like he had wanted her to say something else. "Don't worry, I'll have Chewy sleep between us."

"Oh?"

"Yeah, he is a bit of the jealous kind. He won't allow for any of your shenanigans." He gave a little laugh as he stood up and waited for her to stand.

"I'm not worried about *my* shenanigans," she said, shooting him a look as she stood up.

SWIFTWATER ENEMIES

DANICA WINTERS

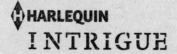

To my kiddos,
Keep stoking the fires in your souls.

This book and all those in this series wouldn't have been possible
without my strong support team at Harlequin. They constantly
strive to keep me growing as an author while making each book
better than the last.

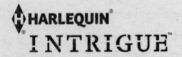

Recycling programs
for this product may
not exist in your area.

ISBN-13: 978-1-335-59147-0

Swiftwater Enemies

Copyright © 2024 by Danica Winters

For questions and comments about the quality of this book,
please contact us at CustomerService@Harlequin.com.

Harlequin Enterprises ULC
22 Adelaide St. West, 41st Floor
Toronto, Ontario M5H 4E3, Canada
www.Harlequin.com

Printed in U.S.A.

Danica Winters is a multiple-award-winning, bestselling author who writes books that grip readers with their ability to drive emotion through suspense and occasionally a touch of magic. When she's not working, she can be found in the wilds of Montana, testing her patience while she tries to hone her skills at various crafts—quilting, pottery and painting are not her areas of expertise. She believes the cup is neither half-full nor half-empty, but it better be filled with wine. Visit her website at danicawinters.net.

Books by Danica Winters

Harlequin Intrigue

Big Sky Search and Rescue

Helicopter Rescue
Swiftwater Enemies

STEALTH: Shadow Team

A Loaded Question
Rescue Mission: Secret Child
A Judge's Secrets
K-9 Recovery
Lone Wolf Bounty Hunter
Montana Wilderness Pursuit

Stealth

Hidden Truth
In His Sights
Her Assassin For Hire
Protective Operation

Mystery Christmas

Ms. Calculation
Mr. Serious
Mr. Taken
Ms. Demeanor

Visit the Author Profile page at Harlequin.com.

CAST OF CHARACTERS

Aspen Stevens—A member of the Minnesota Life Savers rescue unit who is tough as nails and as beautiful as a sunrise. Aspen is the kind of woman who will never be satisfied in second place—or accept being told to stay behind while someone needs help.

Leo West—As a detective from the Madison County Sheriff's Department and a volunteer for Big Sky Search and Rescue, Leo is a man who is pulled in a multitude of directions. When Aspen pushes her way into his investigation of the case of a missing woman, he has a hard time stepping back as the leader, but it gets easier as Aspen is humbled by the wilds of Montana.

Genie Manos—A young woman who is going through a contentious divorce and goes missing at a local swimming hole. Surrounded by secrets, her disappearance may be more complicated than anyone first imagined.

Scott Gull—As Genie's soon-to-be ex-husband, Scott is suspect number one in her disappearance, especially when his gun is found near where she has gone missing. However, not everything may be as it seems—and sometimes those thought guilty can actually be the victims.

Edith Offerman—Genie's best friend and sister-in-crime who has almost as many secrets.

Chewy Lou—Leo's dog and comrade-in-arms. This goldendoodle is not only man's best friend, but—perhaps arguably—the star of the show.

Chapter One

Everyone was born into something, but it was left to the individual to define whom they became. Leo West was born a cowboy, and no matter how hard he had tried to escape it, he always found himself coming back to the world of whiskey, women and hard living. The only thing he had managed to leave behind was the ranch and the cattle, but he would be lying if he said he didn't regret the loss. However, he couldn't say he missed the scent of cows in the midsummer sun.

The call pulled him from the midday lull and away from busywork as a detective for the Madison County Sheriff's Office. A woman had gone missing after being last seen in the parking lot at a particularly popular swimming hole on the outskirts of Big Sky, Montana. As one of only a few officers in the county, he was on the hook.

Luckily though, he and the other officers were a tight-knit group. Each person did their job to the best of their ability, but also did it with integrity. Well…at least *he* did. A couple of the other guys he couldn't be sure of, as they liked to skirt a little close to the gray edges of the law, but he could say that their loyalty seemed to always be in the right place.

As law enforcement in a small community, it came with its own set of rules and procedures. Instead of writing tickets, they regularly gave their local low-key troublemakers rides home on rough nights and instead targeted the out-of-staters to keep their budget padded—not that he would have publicly admitted their norms.

That wasn't to say they didn't arrest their fair share of locals. There was always something—usually gun- or sex-related—that would lead to him stuffing and cuffing his former neighbor, girlfriend or football buddy on a Saturday night.

Hell, he couldn't even remember the last time he had had a Saturday night off. It seemed like this time of year, he was called out on all kinds of odds-and-ends events, like the one that had just popped up on his computer.

According to dispatch, the woman was twenty-six years old and going through a contentious divorce. She'd been hiking in and around the area of the swimming hole, where her car was later found, abandoned.

It was going to be a long day.

Grabbing his keys, he got into his rig and hit the road. By the time he got to the public river access, groups of people were standing around a white Subaru with outdoorsy stickers in its back window, one of which read "Honk if you ski."

He got out, and before he even had a chance to walk over, a woman rushed toward him. She was talking wildly, which made him reach down and instinctively put his hand on his sidearm. It was amazing how fast a normal situation could go sideways when high-voltage emotions entered the equation.

"Hello, ma'am," he said, putting his hand up and hoping the woman would keep her distance.

As the woman lifted her sunglasses, he recognized her as Jamie Offerman, one of the high school secretaries whom he talked to on the phone on a far too often basis. She was a good woman, but she was always surrounded by drama thanks to her job.

"Jamie, how's it going?" he said, his hand falling from his gun.

"Hey, Leo," she said, smiling and nearly bouncing from one foot to the other in excitement. "We were starting to wonder if you were ever going to arrive. You must have been having one helluva day."

He couldn't tell her that he had been working on pulling together paperwork for a search warrant on a possible house where a guy was peddling drugs to the local students—providing them everything from marijuana to spiked methamphetamine. The dealer's last batch had left one kid in the hospital after barely surviving fentanyl-laced meth. In other words, he had just been having another regular day in the office. "It's been going. Are you the one who made the call to dispatch?"

"Come on," she said, cuffing his shoulder, "you know if I'd been behind this, I would have just called you directly."

"You know I'll always answer your phone calls." He sent her a blistering smile he knew she enjoyed.

She blushed and quickly looked away.

She was twenty years too old for him, but she was a sucker for the uniform and he wasn't above using it to gain favor.

"So, tell me what I'm looking at here," he stated, pointing toward the sandy beach where a group of teenagers were laying out in the early-summer sun, although it wasn't quite warm enough to warrant the little bikinis the girls were wearing.

A few of them wrapped themselves in their towels as the wind kicked up.

"I've been asking everyone around here what happened while we waited for you to show up. From what I got, that lady over there called—" she pointed at a woman in her midthirties who was scowling over one of the bikini-clad teenage girls who was chatting with a boy "—and she said her daughter noticed that no one was touching a phone and gear left on the beach. Nor has anyone been near that car, over there," she said, pointing at the white Subaru. "The girl opened up the last video on the phone, trying to figure out who it belonged to and there's a video of a girl in a hot pink bikini playing with a dog."

From what he was hearing, this missing woman could have been picked up or gone for a hike. Any number of things could have played out. If this went as he assumed, he'd be out of there in about an hour after the woman walked back onto the beach from a hike with her dog.

"How long has the woman's stuff been sitting there?" he asked.

"More than three hours," Jamie said. "At least that's when the mom and daughter said they got here, but the stuff was here before."

He appreciated the fact that Jamie had already seemed to collect all the witness statements; if she wasn't careful, he would have to start putting her on the county's payroll.

"Can you point me in the direction of the items?"

She motioned with her chin downstream. "They're right over here."

He followed her down the beach and behind a small copse of cottonwoods and willows. On the beige sandy beach was a neat stack of folded clothes. On top were an iPhone, car keys and an Apple watch.

Odd. He stared at the black key fob with the Subaru logo.

He had a few calls about abandoned items each summer, but he couldn't think of a time when he had found someone's keys at the top. Normally, a person would tuck their keys in a pocket or the folds of a towel, but never out and visible. It was like she was asking for someone to steal her car.

He took his phone out and took a few pictures of the stack. Moving to it, he lifted the black tank top from the top; it appeared to be worn but clean. The shorts beneath were the same. No blood or other bodily fluid. They simply looked as if she had stripped down, folded her clothes and intended to return.

"Did anyone see her go in the water?"

Jamie shook her head. "I don't think anyone actually saw her at all, just her stuff. People have been coming and going all day, though. I didn't talk to everyone. Ya know?"

Aside from the woman being unaccounted for, there wasn't much that led him to believe anything had happened to her. For all he knew or could assume, she and her dog had gone into the water and floated down to the next pullout on the river. Maybe she had met with friends and would be coming back later. Any number of things could have occurred that would have led to this situation.

On the other hand, she very well may have gotten caught in a current and found herself submerged. Drownings happened in this river all the time. People underestimated the water conditions or would get caught in snags. Being as early in the season as it was, the runoff from the mountains was making the water cold enough in some areas that it could have easily been prime conditions for hypothermia.

He clicked on the screen of her phone and the camera opened. It started to autoplay the last video taken, a cute shot of a German shepherd jumping around in the water and then galloping after a stick. The woman was talking to the dog calling him by the name "Malice" as she recorded him returning to her with the stick in his mouth. The video ended.

So, there was proof she had been playing in the river.

His heart sank as the video replayed. This woman, something about this, felt *off*.

Though he hoped he was wrong about the feeling he was getting, and this woman truly was just at the next pullout or something, he had to make the decision. He shook his head. If he called Sheriff Sanderson right now and told him what was happening and preemptively started to get the word out to the search and rescue team, they would be going on a call, and the woman would likely show up, and Sanderson would be irritated. Leo needed to make sure there were no other possibilities as to the woman's location before he called out the big guns and started blowing the yearly budgets for the sheriff's office and the SAR unit.

A woman walked up beside him and tapped him on the shoulder. "Sir?"

Jamie shot him a look like she would have gladly been his bodyguard and push the woman back if he gave her the sign. He gave her a small, almost imperceptible nod.

He tried to push down his immediate annoyance at having been interrupted as he turned back to the other woman. "How can I help you?"

The woman was beautiful, blond, about five-foot-seven and curvy in all the best ways. As she looked up at him, her eyes caught the sun. He couldn't recall seeing eyes the exact same color as the sky before, and he half expected to see clouds float by within them. She was stunning, and that was to say nothing about the red polka-dotted bikini she was wearing.

"So…" She balled her hands at her sides like she was trying to summon the strength and resolve to say whatever it was that was on her mind. "My name is Aspen, I'm on vacation here, but I'm involved in the Minnesota Life Savers group, it's a private SAR unit."

His hackles rose with her intrusion—he could hardly wait for this tourist to start telling him how she could have gone about this call better. "Is that right?" She may have been stunning, but she had already pissed him off twice in a matter of seconds since they had met.

"Yes," she said, chewing on her lip. "I don't want to step on your toes here, or question anything you may be working on, but in circumstances like these, I'm sure you are aware that every minute matters. If she's in the water…"

Boy, did I call that one, he thought.

"If she's in the water and has been gone for three hours…" *Well, the woman was as good as dead. Minutes didn't really matter.*

The tourist waved him off. "I know what you're thinking, but we still have a shot."

It was crazy the number of people who came up to him at moments like these and tried to tell him how to do his job. If she was as professional as she was portraying herself, and in-the-know in his line of work, then she should have known better than to approach him as she had.

"I appreciate your attempt to help me out here, but I've got this handled." He pulled out his phone. "Now, if you wouldn't mind—and I'm sure you are aware, given your line of work—you need to move back from this area."

She opened and closed her mouth as she heard his barely veiled request for her to stay in her lane. Frowning, she handed him her card and then turned and strolled away with the little polka dots on her butt jiggling as she moved.

As soon as she was out of earshot, he jumped the gun and called Sanderson. The tourist was right; there was a slim chance that they could still rescue the missing woman if she was in the water, but it would be close. He and his SAR unit would have to act fast if there was to be any hope of this girl being saved.

Chapter Two

The water scraped against the bank, pulling sediment with its turbulent fingertips. The dirt swirled into the river, making filigrees of mud until they spun together like dancers and disappeared into the crowd.

Aspen Stevens had always found poetry in nature, and it brought comfort and peace in a way no therapist or friend had ever been able. On the water, she found every answer she had ever needed, from when to cut and run in a relationship to when to press hard against the banks and dig until she got what she wanted.

Staring at the muddy eddies, Aspen felt as though it was time. It had been two weeks, and after having watched the headlines in Big Sky, she had found that as of yet, no one had recovered the missing girl or her remains.

She pressed the earbud into her ear and made the call she had known needed to happen, but she had been putting it off for the last few days while she had been training on the Minnesota River with the rest of her unit.

Staring out at the bluffs as she put down the anchor on her boat, she leaned against the raft and tapped the name she had saved into her contact list, Cindy DesChamps—right beside Detective Leo West. The thought of calling him had made her stomach ache ever since their first run-in.

West was a handsome man… Well, if pushed to tell the *truth*, that was an incredible understatement. There was just something about a man in a Sam Browne belt and uniform with the patches creased and a straight gig line that made her entire body clench. And he hadn't made her just clench, he had made her so nervous that she hadn't even acted like her normally confident self—and she had been kicking herself for her mousiness ever since leaving the riverbank.

She wasn't ready to talk to him. Besides, it was easier to just go over his head—it wasn't like she could make things any better between them. She'd already burned that bridge.

Cindy was the director of the Big Sky Search and Rescue team, and as far as Aspen knew, she wasn't going to know this phone call was on the horizon—which meant she very well could be met with a cold shoulder and some ruffled feathers. Yet, she was going to utilize her unit's time and resources to help them; if Cindy cut her off it would not only be bad press, but detrimental in any future attempts to collaborate.

She hated making these phone calls; often departments felt as though her team was invading their territory—especially when they were being paid by private parties or families of victims. As much as she disliked the calls, sometimes upsetting a group of people was just a step in getting her job done and answering a family's questions—they needed answers about the status of loved ones more than egos needed to be assuaged.

Those answers, the ones between life and death and the pain that came from carrying the weight of them, were something she knew entirely too well. Her father's body had never been found. The last time anyone had seen him, he had been ice fishing on Lake Winnie. No one had witnessed him falling through the ice, and no one had even known he had slipped below until he didn't come home that night.

Her mother had been distraught at learning that her husband had disappeared, and Aspen had given up her position as the oldest child and was suddenly thrown into the role of matriarch. Her three younger siblings, Milly and Miles, the twins, and Rebecca, had been too young to really know the full impact of the loss. As they grew older, they had come to understand the costs to the family when Aspen had been the only one taking them to and from basketball and softball practices, and the only one who showed up for games.

Their mother had sunk deeper and deeper into the bottle until her grandparents, two of the biggest saints on the planet, had taken them in and helped to continue to raise them. If it hadn't been for Nana and Pops, she would have probably still been working as a waitress in the diner at Tall Pines Resort after getting married at eighteen to some fisherman who had come in for a beer and left with her on his arm.

As it was, being twenty-nine, a certified diver, single and definitely not looking for a relationship, she had a life that wouldn't have been possible without them. She owned who she was and everything she had achieved to them. Every choice now, every attempt to right the wrongs of her and her parents' pasts was in their honor.

The phone rang as soon as she pressed Cindy's name. Hopefully, this phone call wouldn't cause too many waves and Cindy would see this as her attempt to keep things amicable. This really was a humanitarian call, not an attempt to make anyone feel inept.

The woman answered. "Hello?"

"Hey, Cindy, this is Aspen Stevens from the Minnesota Life Savers."

There was a long exhale on the other end of the line. "Hi." The woman already sounded confused. "How can I help you?"

"I'm reaching out about the recent missing woman in your county. My team and I have been in contact with Genie Manos's family, and they were hoping we could help search for their daughter," she said, her words coming out faster than she would have liked in order to maintain some level of professionalism. "Of course, we would love to work in conjunction with your organization and local law enforcement— as much as law and need require."

"I have no doubts that the Manos family called you in to help locate their missing daughter, Genevieve." There was the sound of ropes being tightened in the background. The woman must be working. "You should know, this family...they are *something*. They are gunning for Genie's estranged husband. I get that money is money and you are working for a profit, but between the water conditions and the family's dynamics, you are probably better off staying in Minnesota."

She held no doubts as to the emotional turmoil the family must have been going through because of the disappearance of their daughter. The Manoses were oil people out of the Texas Panhandle and were deep-pocketed, but she found herself still offended that Cindy would think that she was merely taking this job to get a paycheck.

"I believe you as to the water conditions. I was visiting your state and was actually on the same beach just hours after she went missing. I talked to the officer in charge of the scene."

"Oh," Cindy said, her voice dropping low. "That was *you*. I shouldn't be surprised."

"I've been following the case since I left, as well as the watershed and CFS reports online. Looks like things are moving a little fast over there, but we are hoping to use some new equipment and see what kind of information we can pull to help find our girl."

"Regardless of what the Manoses have undoubtedly reported to you, we have been pulling out all the stops on this assignment, but as it stands right now, we can't even say with complete certainty Ms. Manos is in the water. A lot of questions have yet to be answered in regards to her disappearance."

She had never heard a more polite *Kiss off and let us do our jobs* than the one Cindy had just given her.

Aspen sucked in a long breath, trying to pick and choose just the right words to keep things civil. "Cindy, my team and I would love to work with yours. Maybe you'd like to check out our gear and take us down the river. Who knows? Maybe we can all get something out of this to help our teams. I know we could definitely use more active training scenarios."

There was a pause. "Actually, I do try to get our people on the water as much as possible. It's been a late runoff this season so we are just hitting peak flows, and that means it's going to be some of the harshest water conditions of the year. It's a dangerous time to train, and any day it will be too rough to even get out there until the water recedes and the cubic feet per second, or CFS, is lower."

"We have been paid to work for one week by the Manos family. I'm sure the water will be fine while we are there. During our time in Montana, I would like to help close this case and get answers not only for the family but for your team as well. I know how trying these types of events can be for *everyone* involved."

"Trying doesn't even begin to cut it. The Manos family has been calling us several times a day. They rented a condo in town, and they have been a nearly constant presence at the sheriff's office, according to Detective West and Sheriff Sanderson."

If she was the parent of the missing girl, she couldn't say she would be doing the same thing—if it was her child, she wouldn't have been spending time dealing with law enforcement when she could have been spending that same time searching.

"I'd be more than happy to help control the dynamics with the family while my team is there, if you'd be on board with our search."

"I appreciate that you are trying to help me think I have a choice in your coming out here. Truly," Cindy said with a sigh. "Of course, you are welcome to come out, we want Genie to be found just as much as her family."

"I look forward to working this together, as a team."

Cindy chuckled. "Just so you know, your buddy Leo is a coordinator for the sheriff's office with SAR. From what he told me about you, I'm not sure he may be as welcoming as the rest. Please take him with a grain of salt."

"It will take a lot more than a grain, I'm sure, but I've had more than my fair share of handling men like him."

There were the sounds of ropes again in the background, and Aspen's oar shifted as the river's current pulled at her boat.

"Don't get me wrong," Cindy said, sounding a bit winded. "He is a good man, but he takes time to warm up."

"I'll bring a blanket and canister of salt," Aspen said, trying to laugh, though the knot in her gut tightened.

Everything about this call-out was going to be a struggle, none more so than the fight she was likely to find with the handsome detective.

Chapter Three

Cindy had been vague when she'd called the team out to work the river. Over the last two weeks, Leo and his team had been up and down it, watching the banks and hoping to find Genie's remains. As it stood, all they had were her clothes, her car—which had been clean when they searched—and her parents breathing down their necks.

When he arrived at the SAR building, there was already a variety of vehicles parked outside—one with out-of-state plates. Cindy was leaning against the back of her pickup, tapping away on her phone, but she looked up as he parked on the street.

She gave him a tip of the head as he jogged across the road.

He came to a stop in front of her, adjusting the front of his uniform and his vest. "Don't tell me you let some out-of-stater take my parking spot."

She tilted her head back with a hard laugh. "Oh, man, this is going to go just about as well as I assumed."

"What are you talking about?" he asked, thrusting his thumbs under the edge of his vest.

Like a bell had rung to release the circus animals, the door to the building opened and his team and a guy he didn't recognize came strolling out. Last, but not least, was a woman. She was blond and strutted out the door like she owned the place. There was something about her that he recognized, but he couldn't quite place her.

"Detective West," Cindy began, "this is the team the Manos family called in to privately conduct a search for their missing daughter."

She had mentioned there was another team coming, but he hadn't expected them to arrive so quickly, or with so many in tow.

The woman walked toward him and extended her hand. "We have met before, Detective. My name is Aspen Stevens."

He stared into her blue eyes, the same color as the summer sky. He jerked his hand back, almost violently.

It couldn't be.

"What are you doing here?"

Cindy cleared her throat. "She is the director of the Minnesota Life Savers group. She and her teammate Chad are here with their special equipment. They are here not only as paid employees of the Manos family, but they are our guests as well. Please remember that when you are speaking to them."

He took the ego check straight to the chin. Admittedly, with such a warm welcome, he had that one coming.

"It's okay," Aspen said, gently putting her hand on Cindy's arm like they were longtime friends.

It shouldn't have, but the simple action put his teeth on edge... That was until Aspen smiled at him. As beautiful and piercing as her eyes were, they were nothing in comparison to the brilliance of her smile. She was more beautiful than any woman he had ever seen, and for a moment he almost forgot that he didn't like her and that she was here to do his job for him—a job that apparently the Manoses thought he was incapable of performing.

He couldn't really blame the family, though. They were going through what would be the hardest and most traumatic period in their life. They may have just lost a daughter.

Leo had been the first one to talk to Genie's parents when they'd arrived in Montana. Her father, John, had a thousand questions, but there was only a handful of information he could legally give the man as there were some major underlying questions Leo and his supervisors had in regard to why the woman had been on the beach that day.

Genie's mother, Kitty, hadn't been satisfied with any of their answers.

Leo didn't look forward to taking on their questions again.

Maybe it was a good thing there was an extra set of hands to help with the search. If he could get this woman's body or location, then the family would have the answers they clearly needed.

"Detective," Aspen said, pulling him out of his whirlpool of thoughts.

He nodded.

"We are here to help you. We do not intend to step in on any ongoing investigation that you may be controlling, but we would like to help bring Genie home."

"You, your team and mine… We all know that the chances this woman is still alive are slim." He exhaled, hating that he had to be the one to speak what they all knew was likely the truth. "I don't wish to be crass or disillusion the family. I've spoken to the father, but he isn't ready to hear me. I would appreciate it if you prepared them for the worst. We don't want them to have unrealistic expectations."

Aspen looked down at the ground. The man who was standing behind her stepped forward like he was coming to her aid. She put up her hand, stopping the man before he could continue his advance. "Detective, we will talk to the family and reiterate your feelings. I agree that if Genie is in the water, that she is deceased."

He nodded. "At this time, I believe she is in the water, but again, this is a matter that is still being looked into."

"Did you call in any partner agencies to help with your search?" the man standing behind Aspen asked.

Cindy's lip quivered in a near snarl as she turned to the man. "We have been running the river. Working the banks and doing what any great team would do. We have people searching the land as well. So far, we haven't found anything that would indicate a need to reach out for additional assistance."

"I heard you only have, like, four deputies in your department," the man continued, looking over at Leo.

His teeth nearly cracked under the pressure as he set his jaw.

Aspen shook her head at the man speaking. "Chad, why don't you go inside, and we will go over this case in a way that makes our hosts more comfortable? Cindy, would you mind giving us a moment?" she asked, motioning toward Leo.

Cindy shot him a look, but he gave her a nod to let her know it was okay for her to escape the hotbed. "If you want to hook up the rafts and get them ready, I'll talk to Sanderson. I'm sure he will give us the thumbs-up to hit the water."

"On it, but I'll wait for Sanderson before I line up the troops." Cindy walked toward the door and waited as Chad made his way inside, Chad going in last and sending him a look that he desperately wanted to punch off his face.

Aspen waited for the door to click shut before she turned to him. "Look, Detective, I'm sorry about that. Chad is a retired marine, and he can get a little... *heated*."

He didn't mind someone who was passionate about their work, but he did hate when someone came in and started stomping on the feet of everyone around them. "I understand that we can't always control the people we work with." He paused. "I hope you know I am having a hard time with you being here."

"Me or *me*?" She pointed at her chest, reminding him of her red polka-dot bikini.

"Your being here makes me wonder how much this family did in getting you out here. Obviously, you called them."

She glanced down at her feet, caught.

"Just like I thought," he continued. "I'm not upset *you* are here, but I'm more than surprised."

She looked back up at him. This time the light played in her eyes and made them seem slightly darker, almost the color of a heat-treated sapphire. "I hope you know I don't have anything against you."

The only thing he wanted to have against him was her.

No. I can't start thinking about her like this, he corrected himself.

"If you did, I'd be happy to prove to you otherwise," he said. "My team is great and we work our asses off, but that being said we are always open to learning opportunities."

Especially at the hands of a beautiful woman.

"Detective—"

"Call me Leo," he said, correcting her.

"Leo, we can get along and be friends or I can throw you out of my boat." She said his name with a smile. "Don't make me throw you in the river."

Chapter Four

Chad cranked the winch on the trailer tight, locking the teeth in place. The raft was prepped and ready to run the rapids. All Aspen needed now was to make the call to Leo and let him know they were on time and ready to meet.

After she had met with him yesterday, she had spent the night on the couch of her rented house thinking about how he had reacted when he'd first seen her.

What are you doing here? His words rattled against her ribs like a baton against jail bars. *Thump, thump, thump.* Each word hit her and left its mark on her flesh.

She couldn't be hurt by it though; she had known he wouldn't like her coming into his territory and stepping on his toes—he hadn't liked it when they'd first met, either. If anything, he just had an icy exterior, one she would have to take her time to chisel through.

If anything, he looked *tired.* Maybe it was that and just the shock that had produced the undesirable first reaction. She had to give him a pass and put her ego to the side, just as he had.

Her phone pinged with a message from him, like

he must have felt that she was thinking about him. Or had he just been thinking about her?

She moved to answer it, but it started to ring. "Hello?"

"Aspen?" His voice sounded like velvet, rich and textured with his deep baritone.

"How's it going? You ready for this fun?" she said, trying not to sound too excited to be hearing from him.

"I'm calling to let you know that Genie's dad just showed up in my office. He was asking that we bring him along when we hit the water today. I have told him that due to safety and liability concerns, we can't have him on our boats."

She pinched the bridge of her nose and turned away from the raft as Chad opened his mouth, likely to ask her who was calling. She didn't need him trying to corral her right now.

"I'm sure that Genie's father took that news well." She gave an exasperated sigh. "What did he say?"

"It went about as well as a goose in a jet engine."

"Does he know anything about where we will be launching from?" she asked, trying to plan ahead and avoid any potential problems arising with the irate man.

"That is why I'm calling you. He's your client, right?"

She swallowed the lump that was forming in her throat. "He is."

"Then that begs the question as to why he would

be contacting me in regard to today's search." Leo sounded annoyed, rightfully so.

"You, of all people, should know that controlling distraught family members is nearly impossible." She couldn't make sense of the embarrassment that was rising within her.

John Manos had acted on his own accord; him calling Leo and driving spurs into his ass wasn't her fault. She hadn't given him any superfluous information about her activities, and when she had last spoken to him, he and his wife had seemed on board when she had briefed them on the search plan. Yet, going around her now made her look like she was inept. Why couldn't this family just let her do her job unobstructed and without creating more problems?

"Oh, I get it," Leo said, but as much as he proclaimed understanding, his tone didn't convey any empathy for her tenuous position.

"I will go ahead and give Mr. Manos a call," she said, trying to recover some of her professionalism before Leo saw her as just some fly-by-night who was trying to profit on the back of other people's tragedies.

"Thanks," he said. "I'll meet you down at the launch in thirty." He hung up the phone without saying goodbye.

Running her hand over her hair to sweep back any strands that had been blown about thanks to the whirlwind that had just ripped through her life, she placed the call. She climbed into the truck and motioned for Chad to get moving toward the launch.

Chad put the truck in gear and the men in the back seat sat quietly as she pointed at her phone.

Mr. Manos answered on the first ring. "This is unacceptable," he said with a perceptible snarl.

Hello to you, too, she thought.

"What is that, Mr. Manos?" she asked, in an attempt to let him air his grievances in a way she could hear him, deal with them and de-escalate.

"I hired you—"

"This being a SAR-related event, we cannot have you join us on the boats due to liability issues. Insurance would not cover if something happened to you," she interrupted, not letting him continue down his entitlement tirade.

"I will pay for the damned insurance to go. I'm not being left on the bank. I've had enough waiting."

She could certainly understand his point of view, but that didn't change the fact that he couldn't do as he wished.

"Sir, have you had any whitewater experience?" she asked, leading him.

There was a pause. "I went on a rafting trip when I was a kid."

"Sir, the Big Sky SAR team and I have accumulated decades of experience on swift-moving water. If I thought that you could safely go with us today, I would make the argument that you could ride in our boat. However, this is the first time that my team and I will be navigating these waters, and your accompanying us is not a viable option and may put you and our teammates in danger."

"I don't want to put you in danger, but—"

"I'm sure that Genie wouldn't want you to put yourself in danger, either." There was silence as he stopped arguing. "What would your wife do if something happened on the water? What if she lost both of you?" She drove the nail in her argument home.

There was a long pause.

"How about this…" she said, hoping to offer a solution instead of perpetuating any further problems. "What if we meet up after I get off the water? We can go over any of our findings before any information goes public."

The man sighed. "Just find my little girl."

His voice echoed within her as she slipped her phone into her go-bag at her feet. This wasn't going to get any easier. No matter the outcome, this family needed to get answers, and she was feeling the pressure to be the one to provide them.

When they arrived at the boat launch, Leo and his team were already there and working on getting their raft ready to hit the rapids. There were three other SAR members with him, and a goldendoodle weaving between them. The dog was about eighty pounds and cute as could be with his apricot coat and teddy bear face. He had a collar on that was emblazoned with SAR in bright yellow lettering, with the accompanying mini patch. As the pup skipped along, he made her smile.

On days like these, sometimes it was the little things that made it slightly less painful.

It also didn't hurt when Leo looked up from where

he was working a length of rope on the front aft D-ring to smile at her. The simple action made her heart shift in her chest.

Yes, she needed to get that reaction under control or that could prove to be a liability. They didn't need to make anything more complicated or painful than it already may turn out to be.

Leo stepped out of the boat, turned back and gave his teammates an order she couldn't hear before making his way over to the driver's window of Chad's pickup. Maybe he hadn't been smiling at her at all, maybe he had just been glad to have more hands and she was misplacing her wishes and seeing things that weren't really there.

"Chad," Leo clipped in acknowledgment. He motioned toward the launch. "Let me get my pickup out of the way, and then you can get your boat in the water."

"Sounds good," Chad said with a tip of his head.

Leo slapped the window frame and stepped back, but not before his gaze flickered to her and that sexy smile graced his lips.

He was happy to see her and damn it if she wasn't tied in knots about seeing him. Everything about the job was getting more complicated.

Chapter Five

He wasn't going to take it easy on Aspen. From what Cindy had told him, Aspen had pulled out all the stops in making sure that she had taken this job and gotten herself out onto this river. Now he was going to show her exactly what she had gotten herself into— this wasn't just some wide and lulling Minnesota flatland river; this beast could toss a person in seconds and make them disappear forever—just like he had told the Manos family.

Though Leo liked Aspen, he wasn't going to treat her any differently than he would treat anyone else who didn't want to listen to what he had to say. And he was more than happy to prove that he actually knew what he was talking about and wasn't just all about puffing his chest and being the alpha. He was the leader because he had earned the role.

"Why don't you jump in the SAR boat?" he asked as she got out of the pickup and moved toward her raft.

Another truck pulled up with the other member of her team. She glanced over toward the dude who had just rolled up, and she smiled as the guy gave her a wave. There was a familiarity between the two of them ,which made him wonder if they'd dated. A twinge of jealousy prickled his skin, surprising him.

"I need to talk to my buddy. We have been studying an approach that we want to try—"

"An approach?" he choked out, interrupting her.

"Well, yeah. We've been studying the watershed and the topography of the river and the area surrounding the water. I think we have located a few areas, one about a mile down, where we would like to look a little closer."

"You mean on Badger's Bend?" He motioned vaguely in the direction of where she was speaking.

She pulled out her phone and clicked on the screen.

"Yeah, you're not going to find it called that on your mapping app. In fact, you won't find it called anything at all. Yet, I know exactly where you're talking about."

Her mouth pinched and she looked up at him. "Look, you don't have to be—"

"Yes, I do have to be an ass. Just a little bit. I know what you are thinking, and I appreciate that you did your homework. However, all the maps and the watershed reports in the world aren't going to tell you that there is a large limestone shelf that is exposed in low water. The bend should be running deep and turbulent, according to normal fluid dynamics, but in this case, it is only fast in the inner bend—where it is most shallow."

"So, it's not possible that a body could have gotten held up there?"

"Bingo." He motioned at her. "And why we should take my boat—you have more to learn if you are going to come out here and work this river."

Chad came striding over. Everything about the guy rubbed him the wrong way, but it could have been the way he walked like he owned the river—it was the same kind of walk that the rich out-of-staters had when they spent three thousand dollars on high-end fly-fishing gear when they didn't know the difference between a Parachute Adams and a Purple Haze fly. It was the stride of someone who couldn't take instruction but would solidly try to argue about how they were always open to learning. The dude was a walking headache.

It was going to be a long day and an excruciating week—or however long it was that they were planning on sticking around.

She walked away from him without giving him a second glance, making him wonder if he had made a major misstep in their burgeoning friendship. He had to be real though, if there was any chance of actually getting to the bottom of what had happened to Genie.

Aspen started to chat quietly with Chad and they kept looking over at him with growing frowns. He definitely wasn't making any friends. The day wasn't over, but he had a feeling that he would have a complete anti-Leo fan club by the end. The idea didn't really sit well with him, but he was here to find the missing woman—nothing more and nothing less.

"Come on, Chewy Lou, let's hit the boat," he said, calling his dog.

The pup beelined to him, wagging his tail and nearly hopping in excitement at the prospect of going on an adventure on the water. He loved his dog, and though he was only a couple of years old, he had already proven to be one of the most intelligent and easily trainable pups he had ever owned. The dog was all love and driven by praise—though the occasional piece of jerky was always welcome.

Chewy came over to him and dropped to his haunches, waiting for his next command. Leo walked over to his pickup with Chewy at his heel, and he grabbed the dog's PFD out. The personal floatation device fit snuggly over Chewy's body, but he didn't seem to mind too much as he always knew that when the PFD came out, fun was about to be had.

"Are you excited, buddy?" he whispered, clipping the last buckle into place and tousling the fur on the pup's head.

Chewy wagged his tail wildly and took his hand in his mouth in what he lovingly referred to as the dog's "mouth hug." It was a habit he was aware he should have broken, but it was so endearing and sweet-natured that he couldn't bring himself to tell the dog "No." Just like everything else his sidekick did, this little action was all about love.

"That's what I thought," he said, scratching behind the dog's ear. "You gonna ride with me or are you going to go with Aspen? She's pretty, huh?" He chuckled, looking at the dog like he was just another person in this little conversation.

Chewy tilted his head, flicking his ear up in his best attempt to show he was the cutest animal on the planet.

"Yeah, she is going to fall for that look. Don't you dare think you are going home with her tonight—at least not without me," he teased. An unwelcome heat moved up into his face.

I can't even joke with the dog about having a night with Aspen... What is wrong with me?

He ran his hand over his face, trying to scrub his thoughts and the embarrassment he was feeling from his features.

Cindy was standing by the boat with fellow SAR teammates Steve and Smash. They looked at him as he and Chewy cruised over. "How's it going? We ready to launch?" he asked, hoping that there was no remaining unruly color in his cheeks that could give even a whisper of his thoughts away.

Cindy nodded. "Everything is in order and the throw bags are ready for use if we need them. I made sure we also have an extra set of radios for their raft. Why don't you take Aspen and I'll captain their boat."

"Great." He loved rolling up and having a team that had everything in place and ready to rock and roll. "You okay running their boat? You can have ours instead, if it makes you more comfortable."

She frowned for a second, likely thinking about

taking on the challenge of steering a boat that she wasn't used to down a river that would be questionable thanks to water conditions. Yet, she was a trouper, and a smile broke over her features. "I'm on it. I have Steve going with us. He's always been one of our strongest rowers if I get in a pinch. We are going to have to move a little slow down the first mile or so until I'm used to being on their oars. Sound good?"

He nodded. "Whatever you need. Do you want someone else from our team to ride with you as well, or are you good on your own?"

She shrugged. "From what I've heard, Chad is supposed to be good on the sticks, so we'll be safe on our side."

He appreciated her planning for the worst—he'd found it had saved them from worse things happening when bad things happened, which they always did. They worked in jobs that brought inherent danger and unavoidable pitfalls—making lifesaving and split-second decision-making skills a requirement.

Aspen and Chad dropped their raft into the river, taking the time to make sure everything was tied down and safely stowed for the journey ahead. As they worked, Leo did one more pass over his boat before giving it the all-clear.

"You ready?" he asked, looking over at Aspen, who was clicking on her PFD and checking her paddling knife, which was attached to her chest.

She glanced over at him in surprise, as if she had forgotten that she was there in a role of mutual support instead of running her own operation. "Oh, yeah." She took out her phone and gave it a glance, clicking at it before slipping it into the waterproof bag secured to her vest. "When we get done today, I'm going to take a walk along the edge of the river."

It wasn't a question. "First, you're assuming we can be back in time. It's going to take longer than you think to get down to our take-out point and then back here. And second, you shouldn't be running the riverbanks without more resources. If you do, I need to call in more teammates and have them work with you. The river conditions can change at any minute, and if something happens…"

She waved him off. "No, don't worry about it. I'm just going to be searching the waterline."

He gritted his teeth. "Did you do this on purpose?"

"Do what?" she challenged.

"Completely ignore the one rule Cindy—" he nudged his chin in her direction "—and I required you to agree to for this arrangement to work. What about *mutual support* is so hard to understand?"

The softness in her face disappeared. "I didn't know I had to clear it by you when I decided to take a hike, but it's fine… It was just a tentative plan."

"You have to clear anything you want to do in this state…anything," he said, nearly snarling. "I would like to think that with you working in a similar field to ours, you would be more than aware of how dangerous conditions can become—especially in an area in which you and your team have never trained. Montana is not Minnesota. If you or your *buddy* screws up, and we end up having to send out our teams to rescue you, this will come out of your budget...and your time here will be done."

Chapter Six

The raft was heavier than she would have expected given its size, but there were three of them on her boat, and it had a large frame and gear box. It took longer to hit the step and plane out on the water, skimming the surface at the perfect speed at which to decrease drag and resistance while still giving themselves enough time to scan the bank and look for snags and streamers—anywhere a person could have gotten trapped.

Chad and Cindy's team was running river right while she and Leo's team ran river left, and every ten minutes or so, Cindy would call over to share reports. So far, they hadn't even come up on a downed log—at least so far as she had seen visually or on sonar. However, the dark blue water could hide almost anything under its surface.

She glanced down at her phone as the dog leaned against her legs in the raft—they'd been out for at least an hour, and they had to have been two miles from where Genie had last been seen. The bank was so heavily timbered that she wondered how there weren't more visible logs in the river. Where there weren't cottonwoods and birch, there were cliffs of limestone intermingled with the occasional granite batholith.

The dog licked her hand, and she rolled his hair between her fingers. His vest read "Chewy Lou," and she reached over and scratched behind his ear. His tongue lolled out of his mouth, and he looked at her with what she could read as instant love. She could take this dog home.

It was funny, but she had always thought of dogs as the epitome of their owners—this time, she couldn't have been more wrong. Chewy Lou was friendly and gregarious—the polar opposite of the man whose name was on the dog's tags.

"How old is your dog?" she asked, trying to make conversation in the tense silence as he rowed the boat.

He looked back over his shoulder at them between strokes. "He's two. My ex-wife let me have him in the divorce as long as I let her keep the house. Fair trade, in my opinion."

She would be lying if she didn't admit she was surprised that he would open up and tell her about his divorce so soon after he had chewed out her ass on the bank. Maybe he was feeling bad about how he treated her—at least, a girl could hope. Knowing her luck, and her taste in walking red-flag men, it was more likely that he was just bitter about his divorce and wasn't afraid to let everyone around him have a little taste.

The man sitting next to her on the boat leaned

over as soon as Leo turned around. "Hey, my name is Smash. Actually, my name is Richard—don't ask." He sent her a half smile, exposing a chipped front tooth that was so out of place in his round face, it was almost endearing. Something about it reminded her of the little cup in *Beauty and the Beast*.

"Nice to meet you, Smash."

He gave her a dip of the head. "Don't worry about Leo," he whispered, motioning with his chin in the man's direction. "He acts like he is nothing but business, but if you get him talking after work…" He paused, his face squishing like he was reconsidering his statement. "Nah, even then he is still all about work." He laughed.

"That's not a ringing endorsement for him being a laid-back dude," she whispered back, sending him a little wink.

"He just needs a good woman. He has a lot on his shoulders, and he carries it all on his own." Smash leaned back and tapped his chest proudly. "I'm one of the few in this gig who got lucky enough to marry their best friend and the woman of their dreams. She supports me and listens to every bit of nonsense I tell her—when I need them, she gives me answers."

"She sounds like a good woman," she said with a smile. "Does she have a handsome, single brother?"

Smash tilted his head back and gave a long belly laugh, which made Chewy wag his tail like he was also in on the joke. The only real joke was that of her love life. "Dammit if she wasn't an only child. They broke the mold on my lady."

"Sounds just like my luck." She smiled. "Though, I gotta admit that even if she had a good brother, I think I wouldn't like him. I have a thing for guys with egos as big as their belt buckles. It's why I'm still single." She was careful to keep her gaze firmly planted on Chewy's left ear instead of looking over at Leo.

She wasn't sure, but she could have sworn that the boat had lurched slightly to the left, as if Leo had been listening in and had missed a beat with his oar. "There's a strainer," he said, louder than necessary like he was making a point that it was hard to hear anything thanks to the splash and gurgle of the river.

Near the bank, half-submerged, was a large deadfall timber. Its roots were sticking up and out of the water, still full of the sandy soil and cobbles that had once held it into the ground. The cottonwood's branches were dipping in the water like hands, hiding under the wash of white foam that had accumulated around their grasping fingers—they needed to stay out of those hands.

Instead of steering clear, Leo started to paddle upriver, slowing them down to the point they were nearly sitting still at the edges of the flotsam. "You guys seeing anything on the sonar?"

She glanced over at the screen covered in a myriad of lines and bars that indicated the water depth and any objects beneath the surface. The system was old-school and far from foolproof, but it did its job.

Smash leaned closer to her. "You know how to use this thing? It's probably not as fancy as what you and your team are used to, eh?"

She chuffed a laugh. "I think my dad had this system on his boat when I was growing up."

Smash chuckled, but she could tell there was a little hurt in his tone.

"Not that it's bad, it's just…not what I'm used to is all."

"Anything?" Leo asked again, and as he asked, she glanced up at him and noticed the way his arms were straining as he worked the oars against the current. His biceps were so large that they were stretching the cotton of his blue T-shirt. His left arm sported a large tattoo that she couldn't quite make out.

He shot her a pointed look, like he had caught her gawking and was annoyed.

She mumbled her apology under her breath as she looked back at the screen.

"All I'm seeing is the outline of a downed tree. A few hogs are tucked underneath, feeding on bugs I'm sure," Smash said. "No bodies, but hell we should come back here with our rods and hit it hard when we get the chance. Those buggers must be at least five-pounders."

"What kind of fish do you guys have here?" she asked.

Leo jerked the oar as he glanced up at her.

There was that look again.

No matter what Smash said, she couldn't help her growing feeling that Leo really didn't like her.

"We have trout. Though, we pull the occasional whitefish, sucker and pike." Smash turned away from the screen as Leo pushed them out from the strainer and into the safer water in the main channel of the river.

Leo was truly an impressive boat handler. It took a great deal of strength and knowledge of hydraulics to handle the raft as he had just done. An average paddler couldn't hold and move out of such a prolific current, unscathed.

Truth be told, with so much weight in the boat, she wasn't sure that she had the upper-body strength necessary to perform the same feat.

Smash slapped her on the back like he could tell she was beating herself up. "Don't worry. We will find Genie." He turned to Leo. "There was an outcrop of rocks back there, on the underside of that tree that might act like a turbine and pull anything sinking deep. We looked there on an earlier search, but it may be worth coming back to."

Leo nodded. "You want me to row us back?" He motioned toward the log that was already a few dozen yards from where they were on the river.

It was crazy how fast they were being pulled downstream.

"Nah, it's just somewhere that we may want to take another look." Smash smiled at her.

She could tell that he was trying to throw her a bone, and that he didn't really think the woman's body would be in the deep, churning water, but he wanted to give her some glimmer of hope.

Another strainer appeared on their side of the bank, and they repeated the process, working the sonar—to no avail. Their comms sparked to life. "You guys seeing anything of note?" She was met with Cindy's voice.

Smash picked up the handset. "Negative."

After three hours of their looking and mile upon mile of the rafts skirting along the riverbank, the sun had risen overhead, and beads of sweat started to slide down from beneath her hat. Everyone looked as though they were starting to melt around her. Even Smash had seemed to have lost some of his chipper attitude, especially since he had taken over on the sticks.

Leo sat down next to her. "Sorry there wasn't anything on Badger's Bend."

She felt utterly defeated. As the boat takeout area came into view, her heart sank. She made the Manos family a promise to do her best to find Genie, and yet all she had managed to do today was get a sunburn and realize that she had truly overestimated how much they could accomplish in the limited time they were going to be here.

"I am looking forward to going over all the sonar data. You guys do store it, right?"

He chuckled. "No. Even if we did, there wouldn't be much to look at. You saw everything we've gone over and through today—I wasn't lying when I told the Manos family that we had done our best."

"I never thought you were lying." Aspen had known that it was very possible that they would find nothing on the first day and things would continue like this while they were in Montana. She'd had enough experience to understand that there was a bit of a learning curve in whatever search they were involved in. "I have no doubt that you've put in a lot of time and effort. I just think it is always better to have more people involved."

Leo frowned. "I can agree with you to some extent, but on boats it just doesn't seem to make a difference if there are three people or five. The only difference is the weight."

Of course, he would come at it from that perspective, as the rower. "You don't think you are more effective as a team, though? That you find more?"

He shook his head. "I am not trying to be a thorn in your side, but usually this isn't how we find bodies this far out after a person has gone missing."

"Oh," she said, with the raise of her brow.

He looked tired as he lifted his baseball cap, complete with a set of black embroidered antlers, and wiped away a bead of sweat from his forehead. "Normally, with the water running this fast and hard, we won't find the bodies until low-water season. You know, late summer. Sometimes it's even a year later."

"But you do find them?"

He shrugged. "There are many missing who have never turned up. As I'm sure you know, everything runs to the ocean eventually."

"How do you normally find people, though?"

He looked her square in the eye. "Normally, after this amount of time *we* don't. It's the fishermen and hikers who find remains and call them in."

This really was nothing like being back in Minnesota. Bodies, at least those from persons who were involved in accidents, showed up—unless they were talking about lakes, and then it was hit or miss, but diving was a hell of a lot easier.

Her biggest takeaway was that her chances of providing closure for the Manos family were rapidly decreasing.

As they came around the bend in the river, and their midday takeout area came into view, there was a man and a woman standing on the bank. The man looked to be in his midsixties with his hands over his chest and a scowl on his face. The woman was pacing on the sandy stretch of beach and, though her face was covered by a wide-brimmed straw hat, Aspen could tell she was upset.

Growing nearer, she could finally make out the man's stony features and rounded shoulders—it was John Manos. His voice rang out, heavy and burdened, over the water. "Did you find my daughter?"

Her heart sank. Not for the first time in her life, she was going to have lay the lashes of her words to draw more of a family's pain and blood.

Chapter Seven

Leo felt for the family, he really did, but their being
here wasn't going to help matters. As he stepped out
of the raft, he could feel the agony resonating off
John and Kitty Manos like sound waves. In an effort
to protect himself, he put up his guard, though he
tried to remain friendly. "Hey, guys. I'm surprised
to see you here."

John nodded, watching as they tied up the boat
to ensure it wouldn't leave the area without them.
There was no way he could handle being stranded
with this family. He motioned for Chewy to remain
on the boat with the rest of the team until he got this
situation under control.

"We weren't about to sit and wait to hear if you
had found her," Kitty said, staring at the raft like she
was expecting to see Genie.

"Did you find any evidence of her being alive?"
John asked, barely letting Kitty finish speaking.

Aspen looked over at him, almost as if she was
trying to see if he wanted to field this line of questioning in her stead. It was funny how now, when

they were standing in front of the firing squad, she believed in mutual aid, but she'd been fighting team-work most of the day.

"As we discussed, Mr. and Mrs. Manos, today is more about training your private team on the river." Leo watched as Cindy's boat slowed down on the other side of the river from them and waited. Of course, she was smart enough to see what was happening and avoid the fray.

"So, you didn't even look for my daughter?" Kitty said accusingly, putting her hands on her hips as rage peppered her features.

"Ma'am, I can assure you that we have been ex-pending all of our resources. Today was no differ-ent," Leo said, trying to remain calm in the face of hate. "We really are trying to find her, I promise you. We are doing everything in our power."

"It's not enough!" Kitty screamed. The sound echoed off the moving water and filled the small canyon where they were standing.

Her words rained down on him like arrows from the sky, bombarding him until he was afraid that, one more outburst, he'd lose his cool and no longer care.

Aspen stepped out of the boat and moved in front of him as though she were shielding him from the woman's anguish. "Kitty, I agree...it's not enough." She moved toward the woman and wrapped her arms around her, pulling her into an embrace.

Genie's mother began to cry, and he was glad that Aspen was here to help. He'd seen far too many heart-broken parents, and it never got any easier to handle.

Aspen didn't seem to be as numb to the pain as he was, and he was grateful for that—and at the same time, he wanted to push her away from the danger. She couldn't become as broken as he felt. He could only help these parents so much, but he could truly help Aspen. There was something so wrong in him letting it happen to her, to watch her soak in another's pain, which she would always carry.

He couldn't protect Genie, but he could protect Aspen. Yet, this life and this assignment was her doing. She had chosen to be here. As much as he wanted to shield her, to do so was intrusive.

Kitty sobbed and her husband came over and put his hand on her shoulder.

"Mr. and Mrs. Manos, I am sorry we didn't make the progress you were hoping for yet," he started, "but we aren't done for the day. For now, we need to make sure you are safe and well cared for. As such, I think the best thing for you both would be for you to head back to your rental—"

"We're not going to the condo," Kitty stated, nearly spitting at him through her tear-stained lips.

"That is fine, Mrs. Manos," he said, trying to remain calm and polite. "If going to your condo isn't something you are interested in, then I must ask you to please go to the press area. It is going to be set up at the Trapper Pullout. Do you know where that is?"

John looked over at him, and he could see the pained expression on his face. The man's eyes were sunken, and there were dark, heavy bags as if he hadn't slept since the day his daughter had gone missing. There were so many things about this situation that tore at him, and he wished he could correct, but he was only a man. He could only do so much.

"Mr. Manos, would you do that for me? I'd appreciate it," he said, trying to graciously lead the parents into making the right decision for not only their safety but also for the team so they could do their jobs to the best of their abilities.

"We're going with you, on your rafts," Kitty told him, pulling out of Aspen's arms and thrusting her arm over her face in an effort to wipe away her offending tears.

Aspen touched the woman's arm. "Kitty, you can't."

"There's plenty of room and you should be through the rapids. I'm not taking no for an answer," Kitty countered.

"Kitty." Aspen said her name like she was talking to a small kitten and not a full-grown woman. "I hate to tell you this, but if you and John don't go to the press staging area as requested, then things will be harder for everyone."

"If you don't take us now, we will just go to the next pullout and keep showing up until you do. We are not taking no for an answer," Kitty continued to threaten.

Leo pulled in a hard breath. "Mrs. Manos, Aspen was correct. If you do not remove yourself from our investigation area, then we will be forced to call a deputy at the Sheriff's department and have them come and forcibly remove you from the scene."

Kitty glared at him, her hate for him burning so hot that he could feel his skin sizzle.

Doesn't she understand that I don't want to be like this? That I want to make things right for her? Not cause her further harm.

John's dark eyes seemed to grow impossibly darker. "Kitty," he said, squeezing his wife's shoulder, "we don't want to cause trouble. That's not what we need."

"Genie is out there," Kitty said, her tears started to fall again, defying her anger. "Her husband did this to her."

He had heard whispers about their theories of her disappearance before, but Aspen was a softer touch.

"What do you think happened to Genie?" she asked. "Why don't you tell me as I walk you and John back to your car?"

Oh, this clever woman.

"Genie's husband was abusive," John said, as he started to walk toward the trail that led from the beach and disappeared into the cottonwood stand. "As I'm sure you know, Detective West."

"I have spoken to him, but again, this isn't a criminal case and there isn't any evidence that a crime was committed here. We don't even have a positive location on your daughter."

He didn't want John to hate him as Kitty seemed to. He needed to try to keep on speaking terms with him as they were treading on sensitive ground.

"I have read the charges against Mr. Gull, sir. Yes." He tried to sound impassive and professional, especially given all the things he had come to know about Scott Gull since his wife had gone missing.

"He had been physically abusive toward Genie," Kitty said. "He beat her so badly last month that I made sure she called you guys. It was while John and I were in Mexico on vacation when Genie called us. She was incredibly upset."

"From what she said, she was lucky to get away from Scott. He was furious with her," John added. "We were very worried about her safety."

Aspen glanced over at John. Just because he didn't like Scott or what he had done to Genie, it didn't mean the man was guilty—he hadn't gotten his day in court. It didn't mean he didn't believe the guy didn't have something to do with Genie's disappearance, but without proof he couldn't arrest him or make him tell him anything.

That wasn't to say he didn't have a hunch that Scott had something to do with Genie going missing—he just had to prove it, and in that lay the biggest issues.

It was about a half mile to where they must have parked to hike into this location, and though it wasn't that big of a distance, the two parents struggled with the topography. In several places, they had to make their way down and up the other side of sodden drainage ditch areas, leaving their shoes and socks wet and heavy.

Kitty was gasping for breath as they came through the third drainage ditch, forcing them to stop near a copse of aspens. The green leaves were quaking in the gentle early summer breeze, making it look as though the trees were dancing. The festive nature was in direct opposition to the situation that they found themselves in, but he couldn't help but see the beauty in the simple reality of the world around them.

If Genie had passed away on the river, he hoped her spirit would rest in a place like this, a world of dancing trees as she was finally free from the horrors that might have been inflicted upon her at the hands of her abuser.

Chapter Eight

The mile-long hike had thrown off their schedule, but when Aspen returned to where they had taken out of the water, everyone was sitting around a small pile of food wrappers and water bottles. They were talking, and as they approached, Cindy tilted her head back with a laugh at something Chad had said. The sun hit her face in such a way that she appeared as though she was almost glowing. The effect was beautiful.

If Leo had dated her at some point, or had some kind of crush on his coworker, Aspen could understand. Cindy was cool, funny, strong and beautiful.

"How's it going?" Chad asked, looking away from Cindy with a smile on his face.

"Good," she said, with a tight nod of her head.

Cindy shot a questioning glance at Leo, one Aspen wasn't sure she had been meant to see.

"We delivered Genie's parents to their vehicle," Leo said. "It is likely that we will be seeing them at our final destination this evening."

Chad picked up a couple of bars and held them out for them to take to eat. "You guys will be needing these."

Leo dipped his head in acknowledgment, but there was a tightness to his features that made Aspen wonder if he was just tolerating him—either way, she supposed it didn't really matter just as long as they could work together. Though unlikely, she would have liked if they could all walk away from this day with new friendships; especially one between she and Leo.

He had barely spoken two words on their hike back to their boats, but he had kept their pace so fast that she wasn't sure if he was trying to show off. If that was his intention, it had worked. She had stared at his ass most of the way. Yet, at the same time, she'd had no problem keeping up with him. For that, she was proud.

Suck on that, she thought, looking over at Leo as he took a bite from the snack.

He had green-lensed Costa polarized sunglasses on, but from the angle she was standing at his side, she could make out the gold flecks in his aged-honey-colored eyes. The sun had started to darken his skin, giving him the start of what would no doubt become a rich tan. He lifted the bar to his mouth again, and she found herself staring at his bulging biceps.

Is everything about him, from his ego to his arms, huge? She smirked at the inadvertent naughtiness of her thought.

He probably had hot-man-itis. She and her best friend had come up with the special term for men who were so hot that they didn't really know how to plea-sure a woman because all women fell to their knees before them and pandered to the Adonis. If she had to describe her perfect Adonis, damn it if it wouldn't pretty much be this tattooed alpha.

He had to be terrible in bed. *Terrible*, she told herself. *That isn't to say I can't just imagine how good he might be between the sheets. If he is though, he is a damned unicorn.*

No woman was lucky enough to get a smart, outdoorsy, hot alpha who could leave her quaking in the sheets.

"You okay over there? Something wrong?" he asked, pulling her from her thoughts as she realized he was staring right at her and had caught her breaking him down.

She blinked, trying to pretend like she had been looking past him and not staring directly at the outdoors tattoo, with a pine tree and a fisherman, on his left arm or thinking about his sexual prowess. He couldn't think that she wanted him, not even for a second.

Chewy wiggled over to her and sat down beside her, giving her a look that told her that the pup could tell what she was thinking and was all in favor. She patted the dog's head. "At least you have my back."

"Oh," Leo said. "What is that supposed to mean?"

She playfully chuffed, pretending to be affronted by his intrusion into her and Chewy's conversation. "Wouldn't you like to know," she teased.

He sent her a wilting smile. "Fine, you and Chewy keep your secrets."

Chad stood up between them. "If you guys are

done flirting and screwing off in the woods, I think it's time we got back to work, don't you?"

Her face warmed. They hadn't been *flirting*, just getting along…that was entirely different. She glanced over at Leo, expecting him to say something to the same effect, but instead he was petting his dog, who'd made his way back over to his owner, and looking at the ground.

"Yeah," she said, a mixture of embarrassment and curiosity within her. "Do you want me to go with you?" she asked, looking at Chad.

"Yeah," Leo answered, as he must not have seen who she had been looking at when she had asked.

Chad sent Leo a scalding look. "Yes, Aspen," he replied, saying her name like it held extra syllables. "You should come with *your* team."

Leo stepped around Chad.

If she hadn't been at the epicenter of this strange, indirect love-triangle thing that was happening, it would have been funny to watch the two men pose and growl. However, as things stood, she wasn't here to deal with them acting like love interests. She and Chad had their chance, and there was no way she and Leo could ever be together. For all intents and purposes, their rivalry was completely in vain.

"Chad," she said, "I think I'm going to stick with Leo for now. I want to see how he and his team run the rest of this stretch of the river. That way tomorrow, when we come back, we have a better understanding of what we can expect." She looked to Leo who had an overly pronounced grin on his face.

It made her want to slug him in the shoulder and knock it off, though she also found it sexy as hell. She could get used to his smile.

Chad turned and stormed off toward his team's boat where Steve was waiting. Sighing, Leo turned and followed suit, going to his raft, which was tied up farther down the beach.

Cindy stood up from where she had been sitting on the log, apparently watching everything unfold between the three of them. "If you want to see something really fun," she said, looking at her, "we could make these two ride in the other boat together and we could go without them." Cindy snorted a laugh.

The idea was funny, but Aspen couldn't imagine that it would end well for anyone involved. "We don't want to have to start a search for any other bodies today."

Cindy nodded. "You have me there."

She turned to walk away, but before she could follow the rest of the boaters, Aspen called after her. "Is he always like this?"

"Like what? Grumpy?" Cindy asked with a quirk of her brow. "Or territorial?"

After her conversation with Smash, she had no doubt that Leo was both of those things. "I guess I'm asking if he is always this—" she paused as she searched for the right word "—*possessive.*"

Cindy smiled, the action moving into her eyes. "He is a lot of things, but that is one thing I haven't seen him act like before." She winked. "Looks like you are heading into unchartered waters with that cowboy."

Cindy turned and moved to her boat, leaving Aspen standing on the beach with the Clif Bar still in her hand. Standing there confused and at a loss when it came to how to continue their search tomorrow—beyond doing what they were already doing—she suddenly wondered why exactly she had been so fervent in her desire to come here. This search had been in good hands and under control by a team that clearly knew what it was doing. It had been terribly egotistical of her to think she and Chad and the rest of their team could do better.

Yet, the day wasn't over.

There was still time to prove that she had made the right choice in deciding to take on this search.

She had to prove to Leo that they were not just more weight on the boats.

They hadn't begun to pull out all the stops when it came to her teams' resources, and though she hadn't initially planned to break out different equipment today, she had an idea. Making her way over to her raft, she pointed toward the black UAV box that was packed tightly under Chad's seat. "Can you hand me that?" she asked him, pulling his attention away from his phone.

"What?" he asked, not paying attention to her.

It was funny how quickly a man's focus could shift when someone else wasn't threatening to move in on what another man saw as his.

"Can you hand me the drone, please?" she repeated,

sounding more annoyed than the situation actually dictated, but she couldn't control her feelings, which leaked into her tone.

He stuffed his phone away and reached under his seat and drew out the box. "I'm glad you are finally going to do something instead of just letting that guy lead you around by the nose."

She twitched with anger. "Excuse me?" She looked over at Cindy, who was reeling in the anchor and thankfully hadn't seemed to have heard what Chad had just said. "I'm not *letting him lead me by the nose,*" she stated. "I am doing what I need to do to make this all go smoothly." She took the drone box.

"Sure, you keep telling yourself that. I've seen how you've been with him and his crew all day—giggling and crap."

Oh, this is all too much.

"Look, Chad," she said, uttering his name like it was another kind of four-letter word, "just because I'm having a relatively nice day with another team doesn't mean you need to get all snippy. I'm not leaving Life Savers."

"You know I can't do this thing without you, but that's not what I was talking about," Chad countered as she moved to walk away.

She stopped and moved in closely, making sure that only Chad could hear her. "Then what is it *exactly* that you care about?"

He looked slightly surprised that she would have the audacity to question what he had clearly meant to be a statement she would ignore. "I care about you. If you gave me a chance, I'd make you happy, but what I meant—"

"You don't care about me, Chad. You just want what you can't have. And if you can't have it, you don't want anyone else to have it. You are acting like a goddamn kid, and I don't want any part of it. I'm here to do my job and you need to focus on doing yours." She turned away. "Don't talk to me again until I ask you a question."

Chapter Nine

As they drifted downriver, Leo slowly moved the oars, making sure that they safely navigated their way through the little outcrop of rocks that was pushing through the surface of the water. He was surprised to see anything protruding this time of year. The runoff from the high-mountain snows hadn't really started to hit the main channel of the river. But thanks to the warm temps, they would start any day now. It was crazy how much the water conditions could change in just a matter of a few hours.

As it was, the water was starting to get slightly more silt-filled, and the dark blues of the early part of the day had begun to turn to a murky blue-brown color. Soon, the rivers would be rushing against the banks, carving out the walls and blowing through anything that stood in their way, leaving only a muddy swath when the waters would finally recede in the late-summer months.

He'd seen entirely new river channels created in these kinds of months, and the paths he thought he knew would disappear like they had never really existed as anything more than a figment of his imagination.

The drone buzzed overhead, its blades sounding like someone had kicked a hornet's nest. It was funny, but when it came to the Manos family, they kinda had.

At the bow, Chewy lifted his nose into the air. He dropped to his haunches, alerting to something.

Leo stopped rowing and looked over his shoulder at Aspen, who was staring at a little screen attached to the controls of the UAV. "You spot anything?"

She didn't glance up. "Not yet, but it is crazy what I am able to see when it comes to the water depths. You guys don't know how lucky you are to have water that you can almost see through."

This was nothing. There were areas in the Rocky Mountains where a person and their dog could sit in a kayak and see the log-littered bottom of a high-mountain lake. From the top, it would appear as if the downed timbers were only a few feet from the surface, when in actuality they could have been dozens of feet below. It was an incredible optical illusion that came only with the cleanest and coldest of waters.

"You would think it would be easier to find people."

She jerked her head up and gave him a pointed look, as though she was gauging to see whether he had made that statement as a jab.

He went back to his rowing. "It's okay," he offered. "When I first got on SAR, I thought that I could come out here and find missing people right away. I thought I was tough as nails, but this job has a terrible way of humbling even those of us who thought we could do no wrong."

"You thought you could do no wrong?" she asked, an inquisitive softness to her voice.

"When you are twenty-two and rolling around with a badge on your hip, it does some pretty crazy stuff to your sense of self. I was tough, and I knew I was tough."

"You *were* tough?" she teased. "What happened?"

Smash turned around from where he was sitting on the bow with Chewy. "Your dog is acting funny," he said, pointing at the dog's tense body.

Chewy whined and stared off in the direction of the woods to their right.

"I think we should stop and check out whatever Chewy is pulling from the air here," Leo said, working the right oar as he rowed them nearer to the bank. "Smash, you need to let Cindy and the team know."

"On it," Smash said, and he quickly radioed to let them know what was happening and why.

As Leo got close to shore, Smash jumped out of the front of the boat and grabbed the line and tied it around a nearby bush. It wasn't the best or sturdiest location to tie-down, but the water wasn't moving too quickly and he tried not to worry.

The buzz of the drone moved away as Aspen directed the robot overhead deeper into the wooded area. Leo pulled out his phone and dropped a pin at their location, so they could write a full report about the activities later.

After taking off his and Chewy's PFDs, he clicked

the leash onto his dog's collar and lifted him out of the raft, careful not to catch one of the dog's nails. As he hit the ground, the pup wiggled, shaking off the nerves. He let out a wide, anxiety-releasing yawn, complete with a little whine at the end.

"Don't worry, buddy, we're going to go for a walk. You can *search*," he said, using the work word, and Chewy's ears perked up in understanding. "That's right, buddy."

He reached out to Aspen as she slipped off her PFD; she handed the drone's controls to Smash and then quickly stepped out and took them back. "Thank you," she said, looking back down at the screen.

Her hand had been warm, and something made him wish he was still holding it, but he shook off the thought as asinine. Clearly, he just needed to get out more. It had been a while since he had been on a date. Actually, come to think of it, his last date had been with his ex-wife. Just because he was starving for human touch didn't mean he could seek it out during working hours. He had other things to focus on.

"You stay here, Aspen. See if you can find anything overhead," he said, not looking away from the dog.

"Got it," she said.

"Smash," Leo continued, "you stay with the raft."

He gave him a clipped nod.

As Chewy got done with his business marking every tree within his leash's length, Leo walked with him into the brush. "You ready, Chew?" he asked, motioning for the dog to sit. Chewy looked up at him with knowing eyes, tail wagging and his entire body in twitches and tremors as he waited for the command. He extended the length of the dog's leash. "Let's search!"

Chewy tore off down the trail, his nose pressed to the ground as he weaved and bobbed, working the scent.

It was incredible to watch the dog work; it was almost as if with each movement he could read the dog's mind. A few hundred yards into the search, Chewy stopped and lifted his nose into the air as if he had come upon a spot where the trail had suddenly disappeared. After more than a few hours, fresh scents rapidly dissipated and could become harder for the dog to distinguish—especially if there was any kind of inclement weather like heavy winds or rain. This morning it had been foggy in the river bottoms before they had come out to search.

Chewy's pause made him wonder how old the scent trail was that they were following—or if it was a scent trail of a person or animal and not of something else. Chewy had been trained to alert to narcotics, rotting flesh or—in this specific case, thanks to their hours of working the area—Genie. That wasn't to say he wouldn't give false alerts. Dogs were good, but also notoriously fallible.

Chewy jerked to the left, going off trail and into a break in the dogwood bushes that littered the area. The red-barked bushes pulled at Leo's clothing, wanting their pound of flesh in payment for his trespass. Thankfully, as he began to gain altitude, they relented and he found himself in a pine forest. Aspen's drone was still buzzing overhead.

He hadn't thought to ask her how far she could go before he would be out of range, but if she needed to adjust, he was sure that she could accommodate. He didn't need to micromanage her, or this situation any more than required.

Chewy started to pull hard at the leash, moving right and straight up a mountain face. His nails scraped on the rocks as he pulled himself and Leo in the direction of whatever they were following.

As he started to move up the hill, Leo realized how tired his body had become. He'd already had a full morning of rowing and then the hike with Genie's parents, now this. He was in shape, but he was putting on the miles and had no doubt that he would pay for it tomorrow.

After ten minutes of moving back and forth and switchbacking up the rocky game trails of the mountain, Chewy came to a stop. He sat down, ears perked and body tense—alerting.

At first, Leo couldn't see what the pup was alerting to. Everything around them seemed to belong there. On his left, down the mountain, was a littering of rocks and a few hardy bushes and bunchgrasses that clung to the hillside with their concrete resolve, but little more. Scattered around were the tall, looming ponderosa pines intermingled with some lodgepoles now that they were slightly higher.

A few arrowleaf balsamroots were in bloom, their yellow faces pointing toward the heat of the afternoon sun. The drone was holding steady overhead, and he realized that he had grown so accustomed to the sound that now he barely even noticed it when he wasn't directly thinking about the thing.

Chewy whined, annoyed that Leo was the weakest link in whatever had brought them out on this search.

He walked up to stand beside Chewy, who remained sitting but glanced up at him and then back out to his left. As he stood beside the dog, he was so insistent that Leo could feel him vibrating.

Then, at the base of a ponderosa and right side of the tree, he spotted a shallow hole. Inside, just barely visible was the top of a furry head.

"Dude, if you dragged me off the boat and all the way up this hill for a dead skunk or something, I will make sure you don't get any treats for a week," he said, looking down at Chewy.

The dog wagged his tail.

"Stay," he said with the raise of his hand as he stepped off the trail to investigate.

As he moved closer to inspect the furry thing, the ground slipped beneath him, sending dirt and pebbles down the hillside. This animal, whatever it was, had chosen this spot well to hole up. It wasn't readily accessible by any sort of predators that came its way. If it was still alive and capable of defending itself, he needed to be ready.

He put his hand on his gun, not drawing in the event the hillside continued to crumble beneath him. He didn't need to fall while having a hot round—his team didn't need to have to come to his rescue today.

"Hey," he said, trying to sound soothing as he neared the tree in hopes the animal in the hole would give him some sign of life. "Hey, little guy."

A triangular, erect ear popped up. Slowly, a dog raised its head and looked up at him. It was a German shepherd, but its eyes were sunken with dehydration and the fur on his neck was starting to slough. He didn't look good.

"Oh," he said, his heart breaking as he looked at the dog who was barely holding on to life. "I got you, buddy," he said. He looked up at the sky and motioned at the drone and Aspen. Hopefully, it would be enough for her to realize that he had found an animal.

Growing closer to the pup, he took his time in approaching the animal until he was right beside the hole. The dog sniffed him, but almost as if he knew that Leo was there to help, the animal dropped its weak head back down on its paws.

He reached out and gently ran his hand down the animal's fur. He turned the animal's collar; there on its tag was the name "Malice." Genie's dog.

So where was his owner? If he was out here by this river, Genie had to be out here, too.

First things first, he had to take care of the animal.

Terrified for the future of this pup, he took his time until he had the dog in his arms. He carefully picked his footing until he was back on the trail. Chewy gave the dog a sniff, but Malice didn't respond.

"Good boy, Chewy. Good boy," he said. "You may have just saved this guy's life." Now hopefully they'd have the same luck when it came to Genie.

Chapter Ten

It didn't take long for air support to agree to take the dog to the emergency veterinary clinic. To be honest, Aspen hadn't been sure that this unit would have the resources to allocate this level of care to an animal, but she was relieved. They were constantly surprising her, which made her continue to feel like a heel.

The rest of the team sat on the bank of the river. It hadn't been their intention to camp here tonight, but thanks to the delays and then their finding Genie's dog, it didn't seem prudent to keep moving downriver, as it would likely be dark before they would hit their takeout point. She couldn't say she was disappointed. She'd always wanted to camp in Montana, even if this wasn't exactly what she had intended when she had fantasized about this place.

In her mind's eye, she had been sitting around a fire with a handsome man. They would be having philosophical conversations about the stars and the meaning of life. Instead, she was here with a bunch of other people, listening to them talk about what to have for dinner.

As they waited for the helo to come pick up Malice, she sat down on the ground and held the dog's head in her lap. She had tried to get the animal to drink a bit of water from her bottle, but so far, he had refused. She ran her hand down the animal's fur, over his skin-covered ribs that were riddled with ticks. Tufts of hair came out with each stroke, but she didn't care about the bugs or the hair. The only thing that mattered was giving the animal comfort in its greatest time of need.

"You will be out of here soon, Malice," she cooed. "We've got you. You're in good hands," she said, looking over at Leo, who was building a fire ring out of stones on the riverbank.

Chewy was lying at her feet, carefully watching over his newly found companion.

Steve, Smash, Cindy and Chad were out in the woods, gathering firewood for the night and putting together a large wooden and tarp structure in the event it rained and they needed cover. It was fifty-fifty, according to the National Weather Service, and from what Steve had said, in Montana that was as good as the weather predictions got when it came to the backcountry. While it could be raining in one area, it could be sunny and dry just a few yards away thanks to the high peaks that surrounded them.

She pulled a tick from the dog's fur, making sure she'd gotten its head, and dropped its engorged body onto a large thimbleberry leaf she had picked. The tick's legs wiggled, but no matter how much it turtled on its back, it wasn't going to go anywhere. She hated ticks.

It was hard to even imagine what this dog had been through in the last two weeks. It was crazy to think that no one had stumbled upon him sooner. This poor animal had to have been eating anything it could find to survive, which accounted for the bugs. No doubt, it had been trying to scavenge from winter-kill animals and anything else it could get its teeth into.

People, nor domesticated dogs, weren't equipped to be out in the wilds of Montana alone. It was a wonder that another, larger predator like a wolf or bear hadn't come across him and taken advantage of his weakened state. It made her worry for Genie. If this dog had barely made it, there wasn't much of a chance for the woman. That was, if the woman was out here at all.

So many things could have happened to have led to the dog being here—maybe he'd been swept away trying to get Genie out of the hands of a kidnapper, or maybe they'd been hiking along the bank. However, everything was supposition.

She ran her hand down the dog's legs, looking for any obvious breakage, but didn't find anything other than his being emaciated. He should have been named Lucky.

Leo clicked a large rock into place around the fire ring and stood up to appreciate his hard work. He gave a little nod, like he approved. The small action made her smile. She liked a manly man, the kind who could go from stacking rocks to making love in the blink of an eye.

Not that they were making love…or that she was thinking about him naked and her riding him like the stallion he was.

Gah.

After seeing him row all day, then hike the mountain, she had a solid idea of the body and muscles that were barely hidden by his clothes. If she could live in a fantasy world where she could do whatever she wanted without fear of reprisal or concerns about the future, she would *so* lick every curve of every part of his body. She would love to satisfy him and have him watch as she did.

She hadn't realized she was staring until she noticed he was smiling at her and staring right back. "You okay?" he asked.

"Sorry," she said, trying to cover up the fact that she had been doing dirty things to him in her mind. "I guess I was just zoning out. It's been a long day."

He nodded then walked over and sat down beside her. Malice's ear perked, but he didn't move as Leo started to run his hand down the dog's fur. If nothing else, at least the dog knew he was loved if this was going to be his end.

"I understand," he said, sending her a sad smile. Chewy laid down against Leo's legs and closed his eyes.

"I hate this," she said, motioning toward Malice.

"Oh, me, too," he said, running his hand down the dog's side and then giving Chewy a long scratch.

"But there is nothing I won't do to make sure Malice lives."

Just like that, her heart swelled two sizes. A man who put animals first...yes, please.

"Do you know when the helo is supposed to get here?"

He looked down at his watch and checked the time. "My best guess is in the next twenty minutes. It takes them a little bit to get going."

"Is this normal? Your team coming in to help an animal?"

He sent her that sexy smile that she had come to enjoy. "Our SAR team isn't like the rest of the nation. We have a great group of folks with huge hearts. I can't begin to tell you the number of rescues we've been on where we have gone above and beyond. A few months ago, one of our other member's dog went missing during a search and we all searched for him."

"Did you find the dog?"

"Yes, and the dog had found our vic as well. Was sitting on her until we could locate them both. Dog barked to be found."

She looked down at the German shepherd in her lap, wondering how long he had been out here and barking to be found. "Do you think that Genie is going to be around here somewhere, too?"

"If her remains were out here, from the behavior I've seen from other animals in situations like these, I'm surprised that he would leave her." He sighed. "Then again, if she has been dead for two weeks, he might have gotten pushed out by other, larger predators who wanted a free meal."

Nature was brutal.

"However," he continued, "I think that his being out here in the woods downstream from the place they were last seen means that they were in the river. There's little chance he would be in this location from just hiking. He is too far away from our launch, and there are too many cliffs and natural barriers between there and here."

"You think we should get a ground crew in?" she asked, careful to make sure that she respected his wishes about them working in tandem.

He quirked a brow as he looked at her, like he had heard her attempt to make things right between them and their teams. "I think that would be the best next step. However, we need teams still working the water."

Her stomach knotted. "Which team are you going to be working with?"

There was a pregnant pause, as he must have realized that what she was really asking was if she was going to be working with him or with someone else. There was a light in his eyes as he glanced from the dog to her. "That is yet to be decided. I have to talk to my team, get a plan figured out."

Was he being vague on purpose, just to drive her wild with desire? Was he teasing her? Or had she totally misread the entire situation with him and she was the only one feeling the draw?

His handset crackled to life, and Cindy's voice peppered the space between them. "West, are you there? Over."

He grabbed the handset and pressed the button. "Yes. What's happening? Over."

"We have located some potential evidence."

Evidence? The word surprised her. There hadn't been any talk of a real crime, but maybe Cindy meant there was evidence of Genie's location. Heck, it could have even been evidence that Genie had been out here, in the woods, alive.

She started to ask a question, but held back as Leo pressed the button. "Let's meet up and discuss in person. Over."

"Roger. We will start making our way back. Out." Cindy's voice faded from the air, leaving behind lingering questions.

Chapter Eleven

As Cindy hit the edge of the camp, she nodded in the direction from which she had come. "I made Chad and the rest of the team stay with the gun."

"The what?" Leo asked, shocked. Of all the things he thought Cindy would tell him they found, that had been about the last thing on the list of possibilities. "What kind of gun?"

She took out her phone. "I made sure that no one touched it. Doesn't look like it's been out there very long." She pulled up a picture and handed her phone over.

There, wedged between two river rocks, was a Glock. It had dried flotsam caked on its grip.

"Did you get the serial number?" he asked.

"Yeah, I was hoping that you could run it through the database when you get back. Find out who the owner is." Cindy skipped to the next picture where it was focused in on the numbers etched into the gun's slide.

"This is a great find." He hit the buttons on her phone and forwarded all the images to his device and the guys at the office. However, it was unlikely they would actually get them until they got back into better cell phone reception. "And you pinned its location?"

She gave him an *are you stupid?* look. "Really?"

He glanced back at Chewy, Malice and Aspen. Of course, he had known Cindy would do her job right, but something about Aspen being so close to him with Cindy around made him nervous. He didn't know why. It was dumb, letting his emotions run the show like this.

"Sorry," he said. "Good job on not reporting this over the air."

Cindy gave him a brief nod. "I figured the last thing we needed was for rubberneckers who might be listening to hear what we found. We don't need anyone leaking information to the press. If they do, we will have a total goat and pony show on our hands— not that we don't already," she said, whispering the last part as she glanced swiftly toward Aspen.

He leaned in. "She's not as bad as I thought. She's been a pretty good sport, but I think we just needed to figure out the hierarchy and who was really in charge."

Cindy stared at his face like she was trying to figure out exactly what he was thinking when it came to Aspen, something more than he was saying. He swiftly looked away. He didn't need her sensing that there was anything more than what there was between him and Aspen. Cindy wasn't huge on gossip, but if she thought there was something going on between them and let it slip, it would burn through the department like wildfire and he would be mercilessly teased.

There was chopping noise of helicopter blades in the distance, and he turned to see a helo coming around the river bend. He moved toward the water, so the pilot could easily see him and his team, and he motioned upriver toward the large swath of open riverbank where they could land—though he was sure they didn't need his help in navigating.

The helo moved slowly, as if the pilot was assessing the area before the aircraft touched down where he had motioned. The skids move gently to the ground, like the pilot had done this landing a million times before. He would never get over how a helo could float. In another life, he would have loved to have been a pilot like his friend and fellow search and rescue volunteer, Casper Keller.

Chewy padded over to him, needing his reassurance thanks to the noise and activity that was filling the air.

"It's okay, buddy," he said, rubbing the dog's ear in hopes to calm his nerves. "You help me take care of Aspen. She needs us right now. Okay, buddy?"

As if the dog totally understood his words, he moved back toward her and sat beside the starved pup. He loved that his dog, just like him, was always wanting to be the protector.

He followed Chewy over and stuck out his hand. Aspen lowered Malice's head from her lap and took his offered hand before standing up. Malice looked up at them, not moving his head. He was getting worse by the minute.

Squatting, he gently moved his arms under the dog and lifted him up. "It's okay, Malice, I've got you. You're a good boy," he said softly as he tried to keep the dog calm. "You're going to get help, buddy."

Aspen reached over and petted the dog in his arms. "You're in good hands, baby."

Her words made something inside him shift as they walked toward the helo.

Chewy walked beside them, escorting his friend. Inside the helo was a waiting veterinarian. The body of the place was set up like an emergency triage area. He was impressed and made sure to send Casper a thumbs-up in appreciation of his preparation and readiness to help the dog.

He placed Malice on the blue pads the vet had set out. "Did you observe any wounds to the dog's body?" the vet asked as she ran her hand down the animal.

Leo shook his head.

"I think he may be in liver failure," Aspen said. "His gums are pale, and I've picked at least fifty ticks off his body."

The vet nodded, lifting up the dog's lip and taking a look at the nearly white gums. "He is definitely anemic. We will make sure to get him a blood transfusion when we get back to the clinic. Until then, I'm going to make sure we give him some fluids."

Casper pulled off his headset as he looked back at them. "Did you guys want a ride out?"

Leo glanced over at Aspen questioningly. She

shook her head. "We are so close to possibly finding Genie. I want to stay with Malice, but I wouldn't be able to live with myself if I left now and the rest of the team located her."

He nodded. "I need to go pick up the gun and search the area for any further evidence with my team. I'm the lead detective on this, so I can definitely understand your reticence in not wanting to leave the scene." He turned to Casper. "We do appreciate the offer, however."

Casper gave him a tip of the head in acknowledgment.

The vet started the clippers and shaved the forearm of the dog.

"Let me know how things go with Malice, please," Aspen said, holding her hands together as if she wanted to reach out and pet the dog, but holding back out of respect for the vet's work.

The vet didn't look up. "Will do."

They stepped back from the helo, and as quickly as the aircraft had touched down, it was airborne and headed back the way they had come. As the sound of their blades dissipated, he turned back to their little makeshift camp.

"You didn't have to stay out in the woods. You could have come back out in the morning," Aspen said.

Was she saying this because she didn't want to spend the night with him? Or was she just trying to be nice? He wasn't sure he wanted to ask, as he didn't really want to know the answer.

Hell, it wasn't like Aspen had given him any indication that she would be nervous around him. She was friendly enough, but he wouldn't call her overly flirty.

Chewy walked over to Aspen and sat down against her leg, looking up at her like she was the most beautiful woman he had ever seen. Damn if that dog didn't give his thoughts away. Thankfully, she didn't seem aware of his struggle as she patted Chewy.

"You guys wanting to head back up the mountain?" Cindy called to them.

"You ready to hit it?" Aspen asked him, a small smile on her lips.

"I have a feeling it's going to be a long night," he said, looking up at the clouds that had started to fill the sky.

"I'm not afraid of a little rain," she said, scratching Chewy. "I'm not sweet enough to have to worry about melting."

"Wasn't it the Wicked Witch of the West who melted in the rain?" he teased.

"Real funny, jackass." Aspen stuck out her tongue. "Though, admittedly, that is probably a closer representation of who I am." She laughed.

He couldn't disagree more, but he did like to hear the sound of her laughter. "Do you have everything you need to be out here in the wet?"

"Don't you think you should have asked that before we said no to our free ride out?"

He tipped his head. "Fair point."

"I promise, Leo, I'm more than capable of taking care of myself out here."

"I know you are capable." That was true, but a sickening lump formed in his stomach. He wasn't sure what it was that was causing this strange reaction, but as he looked at her, he wanted to protect her by telling her to wait here and stay behind. Maybe it was thanks to everything they had gone through already today.

He opened his mouth to tell her to wait, but then he remembered that she had already made her position clear. She wasn't the kind who would allow him to give her orders, or to miss out on a search.

There was no protecting this woman. She stood on her own feet, and he could only be there for her by trying to remain at her side. Here was hoping he could help when she found herself in harm's way.

Chapter Twelve

It was dark by the time they made it to the location where Cindy had found the gun. When they arrived, the rest of the team was sitting around and waiting. Aspen was surprised they weren't out working a pattern, but at the same time they had to be as tired as she was. Normally, during searches, they were only allowed to work so many hours before they were required to lay up; however, nothing about this search had gone according to their plan and she doubted it would turn around now.

The Glock was wedged between two large rocks as they had seen in the picture. It hadn't started to rust, but there was enough residue on its slide and grip to make her think it had been there for a while.

"Do you think this gun has anything to do with our investigation?" Aspen asked the question that had been plaguing her since she had first seen Cindy's picture.

Leo pulled out his phone and took a series of pictures of the gun with different lighting. Finally, after he appeared to get everything he needed, he took a paper bag from his backpack and delicately picked up the gun, making sure not to touch it with his bare hand.

"Do you need to clear the gun?" Aspen asked.

Leo looked over at her. "Normally, I would, but in this case I don't want to disturb what little evidence may be left on the weapon." He closed the top of the bag and carefully set it on the top of the contents in his backpack before zipping it closed.

She could understand why he didn't want to make sure the gun wasn't loaded, but it made her uncomfortable knowing that he had a potentially loaded gun resting in his bag. The good news was that the trigger wasn't readily accessible.

"Make sure you are hiking out behind everyone," she said, trying to sound like she wasn't overly concerned.

"I'll make sure I don't accidently shoot anyone," he said, sending her what she was sure was supposed to be a comforting smile.

She gave him an appreciative nod. "I'm going to go take a look down the bank. You want to go with me?"

He pulled on his backpack and affixed a headlamp to his hat. Chewy moved to his side. She loved how the dog was his constant shadow, their bond almost as endearing as Leo's smile.

Chad stood up. "I'll tag along."

Her face twitched. "Um."

Smash, who had been sitting quietly with Cindy and Steve, followed Chad's lead. "Yeah, I think it would be good if we all worked as a team." He motioned around them to the encroaching darkness. "Actually, don't you think we should probably head toward our camp?"

Annoyance filled her, but she tried to self-correct by asking herself why she was feeling this way—the answer was simple. She wanted to spend some alone time with Leo.

That is stupid.

She didn't need alone time with anyone. What she needed was to find Genie, and Smash was right. They needed to get back to camp for the night. Everyone needed a break. To keep searching when everyone was on their last legs wasn't just a poor idea, but it was a good way to get people hurt.

"Did you guys follow the riverbank down to this point?" Leo asked.

Smash shook his head. "We worked down from where you found the pup. Everything go okay with the dog, by the way?"

"We got him loaded up and headed out." He pulled his phone back out of his pocket and moved to check his messages.

"Do you have service again?"

"Yeah, thankfully. Casper said Malice is perking up, but they haven't made it to the vet's clinic yet." He scrolled. "Oh, and it looks like one of my guys ran the gun's serial number through the database already."

"And?"

He looked up with wide eyes and, thanks to the light from her headlamp, his face was filled with strange, angular shadows. "You won't believe it."

"Believe what?" Chad asked.

Leo's face darkened, but it had nothing to do with the lighting. She wasn't sure if it was him or Chewy, but she was almost certain she had heard a low growl.

Leo sighed, sounding somewhat resigned. "It appears that the gun was registered to one Scott Gull."

"Holy…" Chad said excitedly.

"This investigation just changed gears," Leo said. "However, I want to make it clear that just because Genie's ex-husband is a piece of work as a human and his gun has been found in proximity to the dog, this is all circumstantial."

Aspen rolled her eyes. Sometimes she hated how law enforcement worked. She was a huge proponent of Occam's Razor—the simplest explanation was normally the right one.

"Seriously," he said, looking over at her.

"We have a missing domestic abuse survivor and her soon-to-be ex-husband's gun… This isn't rocket science," Aspen argued.

"I agree that everything is pointing in this guy's direction, but we still haven't found Genie. It's possible, however unlikely, that Genie is still alive."

She wanted to argue, but she had to hope the woman was somewhere out here just like her dog. "Do you think she would have been the one to have the gun? Maybe she had taken it out in the woods with her?"

"We won't know anything until we find her." His face scrunched. "I had thought of that, though. However, I was told that the last time she was seen she was wearing a hot pink bikini and she left her clothes on the bank. So that doesn't leave many locations for her to be packing."

Aspen's gut ached. *Scott killed her. He did it.*

"If she didn't bring this gun out here, then how do you think a gun registered to her ex would have ended up here?" Cindy asked.

Leo shrugged. "That is a hell of a good question." He turned, clearly not wanting to talk about all the facets of what was likely a criminal investigation.

It didn't seem to take as long to get back to camp as it had to get to the gun's location. However, when she set down her pack, Aspen couldn't deny she was bone tired. Though she would be sleeping on the ground tonight, she had no doubt that she would be sleeping hard.

Smash and Steve got the fire going, while she grabbed her sleeping bag from the raft. She carried it over to the makeshift shelter and placed it on the ground. The ache in her gut hadn't lessened since they had found out about Scott's gun, but the entire way back to camp she had tried to tell herself that the coming days would bring all the answers they needed.

At least, she hoped so.

Leo was petting Chewy, watching as Steve and Smash worked. She walked over to him and put her hand on his shoulder. "Did you let Genie's parents know about the dog?"

He tensed under her touch, like he hadn't expected her, but as he turned and looked up at her, his body relaxed. "No. Did you?"

She shook her head. "I'm not going to give them any information without clearing it by you, first. I don't want to give them any more fodder to be upset with you or your team."

He smiled. "You have no idea how much I appreciate that."

"Yeah," she said. "I am sorry that I bulled into this situation." She wanted to tell him how humbled she felt after today, especially after seeing how hard he and his team worked. Then again, she couldn't admit that she had made a mistake in coming here.

The fire was crackling in front of them, but it hadn't been going long enough to let off a great deal of heat, so they had to move closer to it and each other to feel any warmth. She didn't mind being so close to him. In fact, he was putting off far more warmth than the budding flames.

"How far are we from the nearest access point?" she asked, trying to think about anything other than how badly she wanted to have her knee rub against his, in fact just to touch him in any way possible.

He pulled out his phone and clicked on an offline map. "So, we are here," he said, leaning in and pressing his knee against hers.

He could have been showing her a picture of the moon for all that she was paying attention. All she could think about as he spoke and moved the map around was how his knee was moving against hers. He was tall; she hadn't realized how much bigger he was than her. Even his hands were huge. His fingernails and skin were well-kept. She liked a man who took care of himself; it meant that he paid attention to details.

"Basically," he continued, his words finally piercing through her admiration of him, "if someone parked here, the easiest route to the water would still be a three-mile hike through some tough terrain. It's the only real nonaquatic access point."

"Do you think that if that gun was Scott's and he had anything to do with Genie's disappearance, that he would have walked in from that point?" she asked, loving the way he was touching her.

Leo looked out at the fire and slipped his phone back in his pocket and then gave the dog a pet.

Leo dropped his hand to her knee. "I don't know what to think about this Scott situation, but you can bet that I will be talking to him as soon as we make it back to town."

"I bet," she said.

"I'm sure that Scott will tell me something stupid, the gun was stolen, he made an out-of-the-trunk sale and sold the gun or—and what I think is most likely if he and Genie really were having a contentious divorce—he will tell me that she took it when she left and he hasn't seen it since."

She wasn't sure whether or not she should reach out and put her hand on his, even though all she wanted to do was lace her fingers between his.

"Though his juvenile record is inadmissible and supposedly sealed, I happen to know that Scott Gull was kicked out of Job Corps when he was a kid. Do you know what kind of a screwup you have to be to get kicked out of a delinquency camp like that?"

She couldn't say she really knew what the Job Corps was. Scott was a peach... This was known and at this point, it didn't surprise her to hear that he had a checkered past long before he was a legal adult.

He squeezed her knee gently and then let his hand fall away from her. Had that been his signal that he had wanted her to give him some sort of reciprocal touch? Had that been his pitch and she had failed to swing?

Dating and flirtation should really come with some sort of manual.

"I...uh..." she stammered, looking down at his hand as he moved to pet Chewy. She needed to get out of this confusing situation and into the safety of her sleeping bag, where she could think about how she really wanted to proceed with this man. If he was hitting on her and she had missed it, what was that saying about her? And what did she really want from him? Until now, she had thought him completely unattainable and, moreover, uninterested.

"I'm getting warm," she lied, motioning toward the fire. "And it's been a long day. I am thinking I'm going to go lay down for a bit."

"Do you mind if I follow you that way?"

Her cheeks warmed, and she thumbed through the number of ways she wanted to answer that question. *Yes, but only if we zip our bags together and you make love to me all night.* Or, *do you really think you sleeping next to me is a good idea?*

Instead, she went with the simple, "We all have to sleep somewhere."

He stared at her, like he had wanted her to say something else. "Don't worry, I'll have Chewy sleep between us."

"Oh?"

"Yeah, he is a bit of the jealous kind. He won't allow for any of your shenanigans." He gave a little laugh as he stood up and waited for her to stand.

"I'm not worried about *my* shenanigans," she said, shooting him a look as she stood up. He started to walk toward the wooden and tarp shelter they had built.

Her gaze moved to his ass, perfectly lit up by the orange licking light of the fire.

"Your virtue is safe with me," he said, glancing over his shoulder at her.

The rest of the team didn't really seem to notice him as he walked away, and she waited a minute before she moved to follow him. Chad had his back to them, and the rest of the team was wrapped up in a variety of conversations about friends and family back at home.

She slipped into the darkness, thinking about her virtue. That was something she wasn't worried about, or what little remained of it. What she was worried about was not being able to deny herself the pleasure she so desperately needed at Leo's hands.

Chapter Thirteen

This was quickly promising to become one of the longest and most torturous nights of his life. He wasn't sure who he had pissed off in a former life to have set himself up for this special kind of hell, but he knew he would be stuck staring up at the cloud-filled sky all night and thinking about his sins.

Though he knew he should have run, or at the very least stayed at the fireside until Aspen had gone to bed, he'd invited himself and Chewy to sleep next to her.

About twenty minutes ago, a couple of flasks had appeared from someone's bag, and now the rest of the team was sitting by the warming fire sipping from the flasks and telling stories. Their voices echoed off the soothing patter and cascade of the moving river and bounced off the hillsides around them. From where they lay, the rest of the team wasn't visible as they were seated behind a smattering of brush and a few tall pines.

If we're careful, no one would know we are doing anything...

Aside from his nearby bedmate, this night was becoming something he would have wished for—friends, fire and the water. Yet, maybe it was made better with the knowledge that she was close to him as well.

He listened to see if he could make out the sounds of her sleeping, but she couldn't be heard over the noises of the night and Chewy's low, rumbling snores. Unable to control himself any longer, he rolled over. He carefully adjusted his backpack under his head.

He could have sworn he saw her eyes snap shut, but he wasn't sure if that was or wasn't wishful thinking.

Though he was more than aware of the possible risks in making a move, he couldn't see how they could be worse than the benefits. Especially in this moment, while he was watching the shadows of the firelight as it filtered through the underbrush and played with her hair, teasing him as they touched her while he was forced to only observe.

He tried to negotiate with himself. If he moved again and her eyelashes fluttered, then he would whisper something, but if she didn't have a flutter then he would roll over and forget any feelings or desires he was hoping to explore. Yet, that was entirely too abstract. What if he missed such a fleeting movement? Or what if she was just in REM sleep? There was too much to misread. He had to think of something else.

He swore he could almost feel the seconds ticking by as he struggled within himself.

His mind moved to all the things he should have been concentrating on instead of the woman beside him. Hell, he had a full-blown investigation to get into as soon as he got off this river and back to his regular life. This was only a blip in his world, and he had to keep what he was feeling in perspective.

Aspen wasn't the first beautiful woman he had worked with on the job and probably wouldn't be the last—he had never really found himself struggling before. What was it about her that made him want her so much?

Maybe it was the way she had seemed to go against him from the very first time he had laid eyes on her. There was no question that she was single-minded, focused and pigheaded. Damned if he didn't seem to like those traits in a woman. She was also incredibly smart, driven, and when she smiled…every time he could have sworn his heart nearly stopped.

Then again, this could all just be about lust. Arguably though, lust could be considered as one hell of a building block in many a successful relationship. He'd had more than a few in the past himself. His marriage, for example, had come from the fire of the loins—on the other side of that token though, he couldn't argue how poorly it had turned out.

He closed his eyes.

"You know," she whispered, making his eyes spring open, "if you are going to go to sleep the least you could do is say good-night."

He sent her a wide, wild smile. "Is that what you really want? For me to say good-night? I could name any other number of ways to send you off into your dreams."

She giggled, and the sound was so sweet and almost innocent that he couldn't help but wonder how little experience she could have had.

"Do you have someone waiting back home? Or with you?" he asked, forced to finally ask the question that had been weighing on him since they met.

"No. You?" She pulled her sleeping bag down from her mouth and held it with both hands around her neck as she looked up at him.

She looked so damned beautiful.

"No, but I'm open to the idea," he said, smiling at her.

"Oh?" She brushed a wayward strand of hair from her face. "What about you and I? Would you want someone here or something long-distance?"

He wanted to say yes, that he would take her any way he could get her, but he was experienced enough to know exactly how poorly something like that would go. Even when he had been living in the same house as his wife, he couldn't make it work. There was zero chance if he lived thousands of miles away. Or maybe in the information age that wasn't entirely true. It wasn't like they would have to have check-in phone calls. Now, they had video chatting and quick flights.

She shook her head. "Never mind, don't answer that."

"But—"

"No, seriously," she said, reaching out of her sleeping bag and touching the side of his face with her warm fingertips. "I'm getting ahead of myself."

"If you need to know that I'm the kind of guy who wants a real relationship before you kiss me, I can understand that." He reached up and took hold of her hand and her fingers curled around his. He brought them down to his mouth and gently kissed her skin.

She took in a breath, gasping as he rubbed the stubble on his chin against the softness of her fingers.

"I don't need promises of forever to kiss you," she whispered, her voice low and sprinkled with desire.

He moved closer to her, taking her lips with his. She tasted like cherries and lip gloss, and it was a heady flavor. He let go of her fingers and pushed his hand into her loose hair and pulled her deeper into their kiss. She moaned into his mouth, and he swallowed the sound like he was a starving man.

Her tongue flicked against his and she pulled his lower lip into her mouth and sucked, making him think of all the places he would like for his mouth to travel on her body. She released him and pulled back just enough that they still touched but she could speak. "If we're going to do this, we should go somewhere maybe a little bit more private so we can take our time."

He was glad that at least one of them was thinking with a clear mind. "Yeah," he said, the word coming out as a grumble.

"Give me a few minutes in case someone at the fire notices me, then I'll meet you thirty paces directly west. I don't want anyone to get the wrong idea.

Okay?" she asked, motioning in the direction with her chin.

He nodded.

She gave him another quick kiss, one filled with the promise of what was to come, and his entire body surged with want. She slipped out of her sleeping bag, and he watched her as she moved into the forest. Her pants cupped her ass in all the right ways, accentuating her muscular and round curves. The fabric pulled against her thighs and his mouth started to water.

It is happening.

I'm going to pull down those pants and kiss every inch of exposed flesh until she fills my mouth.

He started to count the seconds, each passing like a lifetime and proving that time wasn't a constant. Time was the thief of joy, stealing precious moments from the best times of life and stuffing those stolen seconds into anxious lags. It had never occurred to him, or maybe he'd never given it much thought until he was stuck in this moment of waiting quicksand, but time was truly his enemy—in every facet of his life.

Unable to stand it any longer, he pulled free of his sleeping bag and, leaving his backpack, he quietly worked his way into the woods. He glanced over his shoulder at the team around the campfire, but no one seemed to be focused on anything other than the conversations they were having in the raw, primordial light.

He and Chewy kept walking in the direction of where she had pointed, but he grew nervous the deeper he moved into the woods. She had definitely given him these directions, but it seemed so much farther than what he had expected. Had she been screwing with him? Waiting to see if he would really follow her into the woods to sleep with her? What if this was some kind of game she was playing?

There was the sound of a woman clearing her throat ahead, making him forget any thoughts he had of her leading him astray.

He tried not to pick up speed as he moved toward her sound. Now was the time he wanted the seconds to slow down and drip by, allowing him to languish in the moments of nervous hope and anticipation.

There was the thin light of the cloud-shrouded moon from above and as she stepped out from behind a pine, her naked body looked as though it was wrapped in a silver glow. If she'd had a halo, he would have thought her truly an angel. She looked too beautiful, too perfect to be real. This had to be some fever dream—no man, and especially not him, could be so lucky.

"Aspen?" He spoke her name like it was a secret.

She floated toward him so serenely that he wasn't sure that her feet were even touching the ground. "Leo…" she cooed, moving into his embrace.

Her skin was cool and he wrapped her in his arms, pulling her against him to shield her from the bite of the night. His body gave his lust for her away, his sex pressing hard against his pants. He tried to hide his nervousness in wanting to pleasure her by devouring her mouth with his kiss and showing her how he planned on making her forget anything but his touch and this night.

She groaned into his mouth and her hand slipped down, rubbing him over his pants gently at first and then tracing the end of him through the fabric.

He kissed down her neck and gently rubbed her nipple with his thumb, feeling it grow hard, he released it and moved to the other. As he moved his fingers over her, she trembled.

Moving his kiss higher, he trailed back up to her lips. His tongue worked against her, and she grabbed his hair. From the way her legs quaked, he could tell she was struggling to remain standing, so he took hold of her, wrapping her in his arms as he feasted on her.

"What in the actual hell?" A man's voice broke through the symphony of sounds and sensations.

She pushed Leo back from her. "What are you doing out here, Chad?"

"I could ask the same of you two, but I think I have my answer." Chad glowered at them. "You have to know you're being stupid."

Aspen wiped at her lips, trying to innocuously dry her kiss-dampened skin.

Leo stood up. "Who in the hell do you think you are to talk to her like that?" He moved toward Chad, his hands balled into tight fists. Aspen put her hand on his chest, shaking her head to stop.

"Don't," she said, straightening her shirt. "He isn't worth it."

"You don't even know her," Chad said angrily.

"Shut up, Chad, and just leave us alone," Aspen said.

"Listen, Aspen, we're here to work, not for you two to bang in the woods," Chad countered. "This is so unprofessional on both of your parts. If I was your boss, I would fire both of you here and now. As it stands, don't think that both of your bosses won't be hearing about this."

"Shut up, Chad," Aspen repeated. "You have no right to say anything to anyone."

"What we do is our business," Leo added. "We aren't on work hours right now—"

"The hell you aren't," Chad argued.

"You are just pissed off that he isn't *you*," Aspen said, running her hands over her hair, making sure it was in place.

Chad guffawed. "I know you think you are the woman of every man's dreams, but I see you for who and what you are. When we get back to Minnesota, there will be hell to pay. And, if I have my way, you won't have a job and I won't ever have to see your face again."

"Do I have to wait that long? Why don't you just get the hell out of here right now? We don't need you, Chad." Aspen pointed toward the boats.

"Screw you, you b—"

Before Chad could finish his expletive, Leo's fist struck him squarely in the jaw and the sound was hollow and slapping. Chad moved to send him an overhand left, but his movement was slow and Leo jabbed him low in the abdomen, hard. Chad folded and as he moved downward, he hit him again with a hook to the side of his head near his temple, knocking Chad down to the ground.

Leo moved over him, ready to continue his attack.

"No, stop!" Aspen called. "What in the hell are you doing?"

Leo looked up. He could feel the rage peppering his features. As he looked into her eyes he expected to find vindication, yet in them, all he found was fear.

Chapter Fourteen

It had been a quiet morning as everyone had gone about their business and they hit the river. They didn't find any evidence of Genie. In the three hours it took for them to float down to the takeout where their trucks waited, thanks to the shuttles, Aspen had maybe said three words, none more than a single syllable.

This entire trip had been a mistake. Sure, the team had managed to stumble upon the dog and the gun, but they were no closer to providing the family with any measure of closure.

After pulling the raft out of the water and getting everything stowed for the drive back to town, she sat in the truck and waited.

Leo had been trying to talk to her all morning, but after last night, he was the last person she wanted to talk to.

She had been so mad at Chad for interrupting her and Leo's time in the woods, but in the light of the morning, she realized that he was right. She and Leo had made a *huge* mistake. They had been cavorting during what some could argue as work hours.

Though she wasn't in law enforcement, she had heard tell of many officers who had lost their job for something just like what had happened last night.

The press area was going to be a pain in her ass today, especially with Chad looking as he was. He had a split lip, and his right eye was puffy. During the entire float out, he hadn't spoken to her, but on a positive note, she hadn't heard him speak to anyone else, either—not even last night.

After the two men had fought, or more accurately—Leo had kicked the snot out of him—Chad had gotten up from the ground and she had helped him to his sleeping bag. He'd promised he was fine last night, but didn't want her sleeping anywhere near him. He had been only too happy to sleep out in the early-morning rain, by the fire, even though everyone else and even Chewy had slept under the tarped shelter.

That probably hadn't helped his mood.

Chad walked over and got into the passenger side of the pickup and clicked his seat belt into place. He wouldn't even look at her as she started the vehicle, indicating she was ready to leave.

No one else seemed to get the message.

The air between her and Chad almost vibrated with tension, so much so that she finally felt as if she had to say something.

"Hey," she said, turning to him and forcing herself to look at his swollen face. "I am sorry about last night."

He grunted.

She chewed on her bottom lip. "Seriously, I didn't

mean for anything to happen between Leo and I—in fact, nothing else *will* happen between us." She motioned to his face. "I hope you know he was just defending me…" She trailed off.

"You don't have to talk to me. It's not going to make anything better or make me feel differently." He pushed his arms over his chest, like a petulant teen.

His response pissed her off. Though she hadn't expected him to really open up and resolve things, she had at least expected him not to continue to act like a jerk.

If anything, he should have been apologizing to her—he was the one who had resorted to calling her names and escalating the situation. Just because his ego was hurt didn't mean that she was to blame. If he had just kept his nose out of her business, none of this would have happened.

Leo walked out from behind his raft and looked over at them in the truck, his hopeful expression quickly darkening. Instead of turning away and letting sleeping dogs lie, he started to walk in their direction. Cindy reached out and grabbed him though, spinning him around. No doubt, she was probably giving him the what for and telling him what a stupid idea it was for him to approach their ticking time bomb over here.

"I don't even know why you are attracted to him," Chad said, like he had noticed her watching the scene unfold in front of them.

Chewy moved around Leo's legs and stood between

his master and their truck, as if even the dog knew he needed to block his advance.

"Even his mutt is a pain in the ass."

She turned on Chad. "I can understand why you are mad at Leo, but that dog didn't do anything to you. In fact, he and that *mutt* are the reason we found anything."

Leo nodded to Cindy as he turned his back on them and returned to his raft. He stepped up onto the steel trailer and, reaching into the boat, pulled out his backpack. He opened up the top, fishing around for a long moment.

Chewy walked over and hopped into the back of the pickup and his waiting kennel, obviously wanting to go home. His kennel was built into the back of the truck, and there was a water bowl attached to the side.

Leo threw his bag on the ground in anger, and she could tell he was releasing a tirade of colorful language. He definitely had a temper, and not that she was justifying it by any means, but last night he had lost his cool out of the need to protect her. Emotions had been raw and, if forced to admit the truth, she had wanted to punch Chad in the face, too.

Come to think of it, why did she have to be embarrassed about her sex drive? That she had made an adult decision with a fellow consenting adult while tucked away in the woods? The only thing in question here, as to the ethics of the situation, was the question as to whether or not they were on the clock while making their adult decisions.

Walking into the mess had not been a smart move on either side, but if Chad was not going to try to take the high road and instead chose to throw her under the bus for her unprofessional behavior…well, she would have to make a point of explaining how things had escalated to him taking a punch.

Looking at Chad, who had scrunched into his seat and was flipping through his phone, she wished that at the very least she had a video of him getting dropped.

She let out a sigh. She was being silly.

Leo was walking around the raft now. He was putting his hands up in the air as he moved, talking to Cindy. Smash jumped into Leo's raft and Steve started walking toward the takeout like they were looking for something that might have been misplaced.

After a second, Cindy said something to Leo and walked over to Aspen's window. She lowered the glass and she found that her heart was thrashing in her chest, though she wasn't entirely sure what it was that was making her afraid.

"What's up?" Aspen asked, jerking her chin in Leo's direction.

Cindy ran her hand over the back of her neck and shifted her weight from foot to foot. "So, unfortunately, the gun we located appears to have gone missing. Have either of you seen it? Leo said it was in the paper evidence bag and tucked away in his pack last night. He hasn't been back in his bag since then." Cindy's gaze locked on her.

Aspen's stomach dropped. The only item that

could possibly provide them with any answers was *gone.* "How did that happen?"

Cindy shrugged. "That's what we are trying to figure out. First, we are going through everything in hopes it was just misplaced. Before we head out, Leo's asking everyone to do a scan of the area and to go through all their gear."

"No problem." Aspen moved to open the door, panicked.

"Thanks, Leo is in a full panic. If it isn't located, we are going to have some major problems. We've already disrupted the chain of custody by having it misplaced. If this case goes to court, an attorney is going to have a field day." Cindy sighed. "I'm going to go through my bag."

Aspen held the door handle as she waited for Cindy to walk far enough away that she couldn't hear her speak with Chad. She turned to face him. "Chad, did you have anything to do with this?"

"Screw you," he said in a growl.

"First, don't you dare talk to me like that, I'm your boss. And, second, that's not an answer."

Chad chucked his phone onto the dashboard of the truck and threw open the door. "I don't have to sit here and listen to this crap." He got out and slammed the door closed.

She had known Chad for three years and she had never seen him act like this before, but just because he was choosing to be a jerk didn't mean that he had any role in making the gun disappear—in doing such a thing, he was not only interfering with the investigation, but he was also possibly making himself complicit in a crime. He couldn't have been that angry with her, or that stupid.

She stepped out of the pickup and walked over to Leo. He was mumbling under his breath as he was lifting the huge white Yeti cooler out of its built-in rack in the raft. Her stomach ached and was still somewhere around her feet. "Leo?" she asked, her voice soft and nonescalatory in hopes that she wouldn't make anything worse for him.

"What?" he asked, then he looked up at her. "Oh, Aspen."

He sat the cooler on the side of the boat and looked down at the raft's floor. His face dropped in disappointment.

"Anything?" she asked, though his face told her the answer.

"Dirt and a couple of mushy dog treats. Want to see?" He dropped the cooler back into its place with a thump on the hard plastic of the NRS raft. "Damn it."

"Where was the last time you saw the evidence bag with the gun inside?"

"When I was with *you* and I placed it in there." He nearly spat the last word, telling her everything she needed to know about how he was feeling about everything that had transpired between them.

It was strange how her feelings toward things had taken a turn for the better while his feelings had appeared to have taken a turn for the worse. That was about right. Nothing in her life ever seemed to go as she had hoped or expected.

"Leo…" she began.

"Would you just look in your bag?" He gave her a frazzled look as he jumped down out of the raft. "Where is it?"

She sighed as she walked over to her pickup and pulled it out of the storage box in the back. He took it from her and set it down on the ground, unclipping the top.

"I can tell you already that it's not in there," she said, waving off the fact that he was about to start going through her things.

"I wouldn't think it would be," he said, glancing up at her, "but I want to cover all our bases." His gaze flashed to Chad who was now leaning against a tree and playing on his phone.

Leo grumbled something under his breath as he unzipped her bag. Inside, on the very top of her gear, was a rolled paper bag. Leo grabbed the evidence bag and turned to her.

"What the hell?" he asked.

A wave of nausea passed over her. "Oh, my God… I swear… I didn't…"

"Aspen." Leo sounded so hurt. "Why?"

Chapter Fifteen

Leo couldn't imagine that Aspen would have taken the gun or hidden it away in her gear, but then again, given everything that had been going sideways between them, he wasn't sure that she wouldn't. She had made it clear from the beginning she had wanted to take this search on, and she had pushed hard against wanting him and his team to be a part of it until he had forced her to work with them. It made sense that she would want to be the one to report the findings to the Manos family, but she didn't need the actual gun—unless she knew something he didn't… or if they were hiding something.

She had been the one to start things between them last night. Had she been playing him all along?

He stared out at the road as he made his way back to town, the raft in tow. He had planned on going to the press conference, but with everything that had happened, he didn't feel like showing his face. If they wanted to be the big dogs in this search, they could have it.

What he couldn't wrap his head around was why.

All she'd had to do was talk to him and he could have given her access to the gun or let her take the credit for its discovery. It just didn't fit that she would have taken it and put it in her things. *If* she had, then she likely wouldn't have been so forthcoming in letting him look through her bag. She really hadn't seemed to care when he'd opened her things, and she'd even sounded sincere when he'd discovered the weapon.

He ran his hand over his face, letting out a long, tired sigh.

Last night, he'd barely slept after he'd struck Chad. That had been a mistake as well. Sure, he had definitely had every right to knock the guy on his ass given what he was saying to Aspen and how he had been treating them, but he could have handled the situation in other ways.

It hadn't done him any favors with Aspen. Hell, none of what had happened would do him or his department any good. If his captain heard about everything that had just gone down in the last twenty-four hours, he was going to be out on his ass.

His team had been eerily quiet ever since the incident with the gun. It was clear that no one really knew what to say to make things better or to make sense of what had happened. When they finally pulled into the search and rescue warehouse, they made quick work of parking the trailer and unpacking their gear from his truck. Aside from the required comms, no one spoke.

He hated this. It was like they could all tell that he was going to have one hell of a long day.

They weren't wrong.

He did a quick check on Chewy and gave him a couple cups of dog food while he wiped down the boat and the team hit the road.

Alone, he locked up the warehouse and made his way to the evidence lockers. Logging in the gun, he wrote out the location in which the gun had been found and the condition, but when it came to further description, he found himself struggling. It was easy enough to simply omit the details of the gun going missing for a few hours, only the other people he'd been with would have known what had happened.

If he put down that he'd made an error in the chain of custody, he was basically writing his resignation letter. The only way he would come out of this still standing would be if the gun didn't have a role in any criminal activity—or if they found Genie alive.

He shook his head as if he was trying to shake the possibility from his mind. He knew better. Her dog had barely been alive when they'd found him. There's no way a thin, bikini-clad woman would have made it.

If they could just find her body or find out what really happened to Genie...everything would go back to normal and he wouldn't be in this crazy vacuum of what-ifs, hows and whys.

As much as he wanted to leave out the real events of the last twenty-four hours, he made sure to include the gun had gone missing while in his custody and later found in another one of the supporting team's bags. He didn't include Aspen's name. He may be upset with her, but if he was going to go down for this, legally and professionally, she didn't need to go down with him.

JOHN AND KITTY were waiting at the press tent when Aspen arrived. Kitty's eyes were swollen and bloodshot, and she wondered if the two had managed to get any sleep since the last time the team had seen them on the river.

"You need to make this quick. I have a plane to catch," Chad said as she stepped out of her truck.

"Don't let me stop you, Chad. If you want, I'll even pay for your Uber to the airport," she said, having had enough of him and his attitude. Whatever he was going to do, well, he could go and do it. She would deal with things as they came.

She clicked the truck door shut and before she even turned around, John was standing beside her.

"Did you find anything?" he asked, his words coming out so fast that she almost couldn't understand him.

"That's what we are here to talk to you about," she said, holding him off until she had everyone together. "Who all is here?" she asked.

John shrugged. "We haven't been here that long, but I think there are two television reporters and someone from the paper."

That was a pretty impressive turn out for a small town that didn't even have its own independent newspaper. The only one who was missing was Leo. She hadn't expected him to show up. Cindy had mentioned that they were going to take care of their gear, but that had been hours ago. They had to have been done by now, so him not being here felt almost like a slap in the face.

Kitty followed them as they made their way into the tent. Her heart was beating fast in her chest as she scanned the faces of the people standing around her. Everyone was serious and austere.

This wasn't her first press conference, and it wouldn't be her last, but she always hated these things. It was one of those events in which there was no saying the right thing, and no matter what words she chose, they would be twisted and made to sound like whatever the journalist needed in order to support their desired agenda. In other words, depending on the social atmosphere, she could either be the hero or the villain, but little had to do with her actual deeds.

"Hello, everyone, thank you for coming today," she began, moving behind a podium the news stations had set up, complete with their logo-bearing microphones. "My name is Aspen Stevens and I'm the lead member of the Minnesota Life Savers group. We are a private group that has been retained by Genie Manos's family to help in locating the missing woman."

She was interrupted by the sound of a loud truck roaring into the parking area and skidding to a stop on the gravel.

Her heart skipped a beat as her mind moved to Leo. Hopefully he had come to her rescue and she wouldn't have to stand up here to face this group of critics alone.

A man walked in. He had dark unkempt hair, which fell into his gray eyes. The black-and-white flannel shirt he was wearing had dirt on the cuffs, and there was a smattering of paint across the front. His white pants were covered with different colors of paint, and the knees were almost black where he must have constantly knelt on the ground while he worked. At first, she didn't recognize him, but as he flipped his hair back and put a hat backward over his hair she finally placed him—Scott Gull.

Oh, no.

There was stirring the pot and then there was throwing gasoline into it and lighting an inferno. His being here was definitely the latter.

"Excuse me for a moment," she said, "if you would. Please speak to the parents of Genie, John and Kitty Manos," she continued, directing the reporters toward the two who would really give them the most fodder for their stories.

She walked toward Scott, who looked at her like she had a wart in the middle of her forehead. Grabbing him by the arm, she pulled him out of the tent and back out into the open air. He smelled like paint, body odor and cigarettes.

"Whadya want?" Scott asked, pulling his arm out of her grip.

"What are you doing here, Scott?" she asked.

"What business of that is yours, Aspen?" He motioned his chin in the direction of the podium where she had just introduced herself. "I have every right to be here and be a part of finding my wife."

"Are you kidding me?" she countered, staring at a long hair that was sticking nearly sideways out from his hat. "I just spoke with the detective who is working this case, and he said that you haven't showed any interest in coming out here to find Genie. Now, when there is press involved, you decide to show up? I don't think so. You need to leave."

As she spoke, she couldn't help but glance in Chad's direction. Little had she known that she would have a trail of figurative bodies in her wake today.

"You ain't got no right to tell me where I can be. This is a public event. And I gotta know what's goin' on with Genie."

"What's going on is that she has been missing for over two weeks and you are suspect number one."

The man gave a mirthful chuckle. "If I'm the best suspect that detective's got, then he's doin' a piss-poor job. I ain't got nothin' to do with her goin' missin'."

"Oh, I'm sure you are innocent." She scanned him up and down, raising her lip in a near snarl. "I have heard all about what you did to your *beloved wife*."

He spat on the ground. "You think you got all the answers, don't ya?"

She wanted to tell him that they had found his gun, that he was going to go down for Genie's death. Yet, without the body she was more than aware it often was incredibly hard to prove a crime had been committed.

Her only hope in nailing this guy for having a role in Genie's disappearance was to get him the hell out of there before she said something she would regret. She'd already had enough of that in the last day and she didn't need anything else hanging on her conscience.

"If you don't leave right now, I'm going to call the police and have you removed."

He threw his head back in a laugh. "Go ahead and call 'em. You may think I'm some dumb redneck, but I know I got the right to be here."

He wasn't wrong, on either count.

She ran her hand over her face; there had been so much drama in her life, and she didn't need any more crap if it wasn't absolutely necessary. "You and I both know that if you walk back in there and Genie's parents see you, there will be fireworks. Do you really think you getting in a fight with them on camera is a smart idea? If you are trying to appear innocent in all of this, or at least like a somewhat caring husband, it would be in your best interest to go."

Just as she finished talking, a truck appeared around the bend at the end of the road—Leo's truck. Her stomach clenched.

Ten minutes ago, she had been hoping for him to come to her rescue, but now that he was here, she wasn't sure whether or not his appearance would make things better or so much worse.

Chapter Sixteen

Scott Gull was a piece of crap. Every time Leo had ever been forced to be around the guy it had taken every bit of his willpower not to arrest him. When he spotted him standing next to Aspen, his blood began to boil. He had no right to be at the press conference. Actually, if he stopped walking on this Earth that would have been just fine, too.

He parked his truck and made his way over to them. Chewy whined from his kennel, but he could stay put for now.

"Mr. Gull," he said, giving him an acknowledging tip of the head. He glanced over at the late-model, lifted F-150. Originally, the truck had probably been white, but now it was mostly rust and powdery cream. "What are you doing here?"

"Why do y'all keep askin' me that like I don't gotta reason? My wife is missin'. I wanna know what y'all are doin' to get her back to me."

Aspen shot Leo a look, one that told him that she was as weary of this man as he was. John's voice sounded from the tent. Leo put his hand on the guy's arm. "Let's take a little walk toward your truck." They must have finally seen Genie's husband or heard him out here.

The guy shrugged off his hand, the motion aggressive. "Don't you dare lay hands on me."

"Why?" Aspen countered. "You don't like it when someone touches you without your consent?"

"What the hell did you just say to me?" Scott growled, moving to take a step toward Aspen. His arm moved upward like he was considering taking a swing.

"You don't like mouthy women, do you?" she pressed.

Before the guy could take another step, Leo got in his space. "Scott, before you do something stupid, I think it best if you head back to your truck. I have some things I want to discuss with you about your wife's case."

Scott looked at him with hate in his eyes. If Leo hadn't seen that look a thousand times before, he may have almost gotten a hurt feeling. As it was, those kinds of looks generally meant he was doing something right.

Maybe that was part of the reason he couldn't be in a relationship. He was a broken man—what most people considered normal emotions and reactions weren't his. Here he was just hammering that feeling about himself home.

"Let's go," he ordered, pointing at the man's truck.

This time, Scott didn't put up a fight, which was good. Maybe he could tell that Leo was losing his war with his patience.

As Scott ambled off, Leo turned to Aspen. "You just had to kick the hornet's nest, didn't you?"

She tilted her head, as she squinted her eyes with anger. "Seems like there are a lot of those hornet's nests just laying around."

"Fighting with purpose is one thing, fighting for fighting's sake is another. You been around this game as long as I have, you wise up—you learn what's worth the battle."

She opened her mouth to speak, but instead she clamped her lips shut as she must have let the back-handed compliment and admonition sink it.

"Please go sit with Genie's family and talk them down from the ledge," he said, motioning toward the press tent. "Don't let the reporters run away with the story. I will be back as soon as I'm done dealing with him." He jabbed his thumb toward Scott.

"You know he has something to do with Genie's disappearance. After meeting him, I have no doubt. I can feel it in my gut."

Leo raised his hand. "We will see."

Scott was putting a dip of Copenhagen in his lip as Leo approached. "I know y'all don't like me. I don't expect you to like me…especially if y'all have been listenin' to her old man and old lady."

"Oh, is that right?" Leo asked. "What makes you say that?"

"That old lady is crazier than a rat. Used to treat Genie like she was nothin' and nobody. Now, I see her on the news actin' like she was God's gift to her daughter…that they were the perfect family."

"Is that what Genie told you?" Leo put his arms on the hood of the truck, the chalky paint sticking to his skin.

"Genie would talk all about her mom, how she'd get drunk and not come home some nights. When she would come home, she'd get in big fights with her boyfriend. You know John ain't really Genie's dad. He's just some guy Kitty picked up along the way to pay the tab."

Leo tried to hide his shock at the new information. "When you and I spoke last time, you didn't mention any of this to me. Why are you suddenly so chatty?"

"Last time we talked, they hadn't opened their big mouths. I didn't have no problems bein' in the same town as 'em, but now that they are tellin' everyone I'm the bad guy... That I was beatin' on Genie." He spat on the ground. "Well, I had to come and say my piece."

Of course, Scott is going to profess his innocence. Is no one ever guilty?

"Look, you and I both know that you are currently charged with Partner Family Member Assault, a PFMA, and that you are awaiting trial. In the meantime, she slapped you with a temporary restraining order. A person doesn't get the charge just thrown at them unless there was some reason for us to arrest you." Leo tried his damnedest to sound like he was being understanding and not amping up for another verbal battle with the guy.

"You're right... I'm goin' to trial. I ain't been convicted yet." Scott spit again. "You ever wonder how that fight got called in…or by who?"

Leo twitched. Normally, the first thing he ever did on any of his investigations was listen to the 911 call. Yet, in the case of the PFMA, he hadn't. It hadn't seemed applicable to Genie going missing. "Who made the call, Scott?"

He jabbed his chin in the direction of the tent. "That old witch."

Holy crap.

He would have to look deeper into this claim. As much as he wanted to buy into what the guy was saying, there were always a variety of sides to every story.

"Did you get along with Genie's family before this all happened?"

Scott scoffed. "I got along better with 'em than she did. The only time Kitty ever called her was when she wanted a few bucks and didn't want John to know."

"You have any proof of that?"

"I dunno. I don't think that Genie ever gave in to her mom, but if she did she may notta told me. She knew my feelings on handouts."

"Which were?"

"You give a man a fish and he'll eat for a day, but if you teach him…" Scott said, puffing up his chest like he was a philosopher.

In that, he found plenty of reason for Genie to keep secrets from her husband. It was common that when a person was forced to choose between family and a spouse, they would side with the spouse, but sometimes—especially in cases in which the families were abusive or toxic—things would go the other way. There was always that draw, that desire for the child to get love and affection from the parent who would burn them with cigarettes five minutes later.

The more he learned about Genie, the more his heart hurt for her plight. No matter where this poor woman was, she seemed to have surrounded herself with the worst kind of people. Genie was in a cycle that she never had a chance to break from.

"Do you think it's possible that Genie's parents would have done anything to harm their daughter in any way?" Scott asked.

Scott kicked the front tire of his pickup. "She needs a little air. This damned thing has a slow leak."

"I have a tire that's like that, too," he said. "It's from all the salt on the roads. Eats away at the rims."

Scott huffed. "Don't I know. I drive this beast too hard. She ain't never gettin' a break—hell or high water. Ya know?"

"Oh, don't I. I've been putting in a lot of hours. Even more since this all started," he said, trying to lead the man back to the question he was trying to avoid. "You know, even if those folks are around, I won't tell you that you can't be here. All I want is civility. I don't want to take anything away from our search efforts by having to babysit you three."

Scott dipped his head. "I hear ya. I mighta come in a little hot, but you gotta know—"

"I know all about how it feels to have your name

ran through the mud. I'm a cop, remember?" He gave a chuckle.

Scott looked up at him. "I ain't said it, but I hope y'all know that I do appreciate all that y'all are doin' to find my Genie."

"You're welcome," Leo said, some of his dislike for the man dissolving.

While Scott definitely wasn't without fault, and he wasn't what he'd consider a perfect member of society, he was a man who had loved his wife. Though there was a very thin line between love and hate, he hadn't gotten the impression either time he'd chatted with him that Scott had hated her or wished her harm. He'd been angry at the situation, but not at the woman.

"Scott, why would Kitty make a call about a domestic disturbance involving you and Genie? Were you hitting her, being rough at all?" He tried to be careful in how he worded his question. He didn't want to lose ground with his primary suspect in Genie's disappearance, especially now that he finally had him opening up.

"I never laid a hand on my Genie," Scott said, putting his hand to his chest like he was preaching the truth. "We got into some pretty heated fights, I ain't gonna lie, but I never once touched a hair on her head outta anger."

"Did you ever make her feel intimidated?"

Scott looked back down at his tire. "I know how the law works, Detective West."

"What do you mean, Scott?"

"I know that even if I got to yellin' at her and we were goin' around and she felt like I was tryin' to scare her, that in this state, I'm as good as any old wife beater."

"So, you did raise your voice and scare her?"

"She got a recording of me on her phone," Scott said, his voice barely above a whisper. "She sent it to her mom."

Now things were starting to click. "And Mrs. Manos used it to have you arrested?"

"Yeah, but Genie didn't even want to press charges. She was gone when you guys arrived, and they just cuffed and stuffed me. I didn't stand a chance."

"If you were arrested, Scott, then it means that Genie did choose to press charges."

Scott gave a slight, guilty nod. "I know. I can't say I'm prouda how all the things went down. Like I said, we weren't doin' real good. I think Kitty convinced her that if she did press charges that things would be easier in court if we did decide to split." He gave Leo a pleading look. "I told her I didn't wanna get a divorce, but she had other ideas."

"Genie or Kitty?"

"Hell, now you know they were in it together," Scott said with a hard shrug. "I can't say I under-stand women any better than I did when I was a kid. They are, and will always be, a goddamned mystery."

Not for the first time while they'd been talking, Leo's thoughts turned to Aspen. In this sentiment, Scott was right—women were a mystery, none more than the woman whose flavor he could still recall and wanted to taste again. However, he held no doubt that between kissing Aspen again and finding the answers to Genie's whereabouts, he held better odds in solving her disappearance.

Chapter Seventeen

Aspen was only too glad to get out of the tent and away from the Manos family after the press conference. Though she had made sure to keep the information she shared to a minimum, only saying that they had found the dog and he was currently alive and in the hands of a capable local veterinarian, she had been forced to face a wave of hard questions.

The journalists dug hard about the animal, asking all about where and how it had been found. She gave them vague details. She and the search teams didn't need anyone digging around the area that she was hoping to get back to again in order to give another search.

John and Kitty had been surprisingly quiet during her press update. They had been wholly occupied by Scott and Leo outside. Kitty kept trying to stand up, and she had seen John jerk her back to her seat at least three times. While she didn't agree with a man telling a woman what to do or how to do it, she appreciated that his actions were helping to prevent a battle in front of the news cameras.

As she walked outside, she drew in a long breath and gave a cleansing exhale.

Leo was standing over on the bridge in the distance, staring out at the water with his back to her. It was a few hundred yards from the tent and about a half mile downstream from where they had been taken out, and she was sure that Leo was scanning the riverbanks for any signs of Genie. She checked the small parking area for Scott, but it looked as though he and his truck were gone.

Thank goodness.

Maybe their luck had finally turned. From the get-go, it had seemed as though nothing had wanted to go her way.

Well, except last night.

Even that had ended poorly, though.

Chad was still sitting in their truck, and he appeared to be taking a nap. Now that the conference was over, she should probably make things right between them, but the idea sounded about as appealing as putting her head in a crocodile's mouth. She had just swum through a pool of them and seeing another one could wait.

She walked toward the bridge, her feet crunching on the gravel. It was funny how here it was so dry after the early-morning rains. This state's climate was strange. A person really couldn't know with any amount of certainty what the future would bring—in weather or in life.

"Hey, Leo," she said, looking over the edge of the bridge toward the river running below. Since they had taken out this morning, it looked as though the river had come up a couple of inches.

"Hey," he said, not turning to face her. "How did things go in there?"

"Fine. I took your advice and tried to keep the reporters at bay."

He nodded in approval. "Good for you. Those things can be a blood bath sometimes. I'm impressed you came out with all your fingers and toes."

"Don't get too excited. We don't know what they will write about."

"How were the Manoses?" he asked, finally looking away from the river and toward her.

"They definitely weren't happy to see the ex." She glanced around, still half expecting to find him lurking in the area. "What happened there?"

His face pinched slightly, but she couldn't make heads or tails of his expression.

"I found out that I'm going to need to look a little deeper into some things."

"Like what?" she asked, not sure whether they were on the right foot enough that he would open up to her.

"Let's just say that everything may not be as it appears with Mom and Dad in there," he said, and as he motioned in their direction, it was as if they had known and they came walking out.

Kitty was talking to Susan Delacorte, one of the reporters Aspen recognized from the meeting they'd just had. The woman was nodding, taking notes about the situation on her phone as Kitty spoke. She could only imagine what the woman was telling her.

"All I talked about was the dog. I didn't let anyone know about the gun."

Finally, Leo smiled. "That's great. I don't want that information hitting the main pipeline."

She opened her mouth to say something about finding it in her bag, but decided against it. There was no sense in even talking about something that couldn't be undone…just like what had happened in the woods. If it was up to her, they could just go ahead and pretend that he hadn't seen her naked and nothing had happened.

"So…" he said, his gaze moving to her pickup. "What is Chad going to do?"

She cringed. "He wants to go back to Minnesota. I think he's planning on catching the first flight out of here."

Leo mumbled something under his breath that sounded like, "Not a moment too soon," but she wasn't entirely sure.

Leo cleared his throat. "Are you going to try to stop him?"

"I can't think of a way to make him stay or to make things go back to the way they were."

"You mean him fawning over you?" Leo asked, a sharpness in his tone.

"What is that supposed to mean?" she asked, trying hard not to be offended and yet failing.

Why would he say something like that?

"All I meant was that…" Leo paused like he was trying to find the right words. "I guess all I meant was that I'm sorry."

She forgot about being offended as he took her by surprise with his apology. Out of all the things she had thought he would say, that was at the bottom of the list. "What are you sorry for?" *Kicking the crap out of Chad or about putting both of our careers at risk?* "You know, you're not the one who walked out from behind that tree naked."

She exhaled again, hoping it would have the same calming effect as when she had left the tent, but she still felt just as tied in knots as she had before.

He sent her a wide grin. "I'm sorry things went sideways, but I'll never be sorry about seeing you step out from the forest. That is about every man's fantasy."

She tried to check her giggle, but it slipped from her lips. "I don't know about *every man's.*"

"Any man who's worth his salt," Leo said, his eyes taking on a brightness.

"Regardless," she said, trying to steer things back on course and out of the emotional chaos that they had become, "I won't take things there again. I'm sorry, too."

"No need to apologize to me for something like that," he said, sending her a smile that threatened her shaky resolve. "You know I'm just wondering whether or not we can both agree Chad had the punch coming?" he asked, looking half proud.

"I think you could have handled that a little differently, but I would be lying if I said that I didn't find it the slightest bit sexy." As the last word left her, her cheeks warmed. "Damn it. Sorry. No more.

That's it. I won't flirt with you again. That was just a leftover."

He laughed. "Put that in the *seeing you naked* category…it's not something you need to regret or apologize for."

"Regardless, we have both learned all too well in the last few hours what we want to do and what we *should do* are very different things."

He moved like he wanted to argue, but stopped himself. "I'll respect your boundaries." He scratched harshly at the side of his face where she noticed he must have shaved after they had parted ways this morning.

"By the way," she said, "I appreciate you coming down to help with the press conference. I don't know what I would have done in this situation, had you not been here to intercede."

He waved her off. "I wasn't going to, but I could tell that you were looking forward to this thing about as much as a root canal."

"Was it that obvious?" she said, with a feeble smile.

"It's the same way I feel about what I need to do now." He looked off in the direction of the tent and John and Kitty. "As you are involved and hired by this family, you are welcome to tag along, but I need to speak to them before they leave." He started to walk, but motioned for her to follow.

"What do you need to talk to them about?" She didn't want to go back over to that tent, but just like he hadn't made her face this day alone, she wasn't about to let him go alone now, either. Sometimes it helped to have someone in your corner, even if they said nothing at all.

"I just need to ask them a few questions." He waved toward John. "Mr. Manos?" he called, waiting until the last reporter went to their car.

Genie's father turned toward them and frowned, and said something she couldn't hear to Kitty as they approached.

"Mrs. Manos," Leo said, giving the woman a slight nod in acknowledgment. "I hope you both found some level of comfort in our finding Malice."

Kitty sniffed, sounding irritated.

"We are very glad about the dog." John took hold of Kitty's hand like he was trying to keep her in check.

"I gave them your phone numbers, if you want to take the dog home when he is recovered. Have you spoken to them today?"

John shook his head. "They called, but we aren't in any position to be responsible for a dog. As much as we appreciate you finding him, he is Genie's."

Their answer surprised Aspen. If she had been in their position, she could have understood their reticence in taking on more responsibilities at the present moment, but this animal was important to Genie. If they held hopes of finding her alive, she would have thought they would want to take the dog in and keep him in hopes Genie would come back home.

"What in the hell was Scott doing here?" Kitty said angrily. "He has no business being around here."

Leo's features flickered with darkness, but the look was quickly replaced by his characteristic alpha stoicism. "Ma'am, while I can understand that you are not getting along with him, he is Genie's legal husband."

"They were getting a divorce. She had started to get the paperwork drawn up."

"Getting paperwork together and being divorced are very different things," he said, but as he spoke she could tell he was struggling to keep his frustration from sneaking into his inflections. "As her husband, he is the only one who can actually make any choices when it comes to Genie and her welfare."

"But I'm her mother," Kitty said. "And John…" She motioned toward her husband.

"About your relationship," he said, pivoting. "Are you two married?"

John looked offended. "Of course we are married. What relevance does that have on any of this?"

"I'm just accumulating information, sir." Leo put his hands up to his shirt and pressed his thumbs under what must have been a bulletproof vest beneath.

How had she not noticed he was wearing one?

Aspen tried not to stare at the way the vest curved around his body and pressed against his shirt. It wasn't flattering to his body, but there was something incredibly sexy about a man in a Kevlar vest.

She had never worn one.

Focus. I promised I wouldn't flirt.

Then again, I didn't make any promises about staring.

Or wanting.

"How long have you and John been married?" he asked, pulling her from her thoughts.

"We've been married five years. Almost six," Kitty said, sounding self-righteous.

Her tone drew Aspen's attention back to the task that was actually at hand, and not the task she wished was in her hand instead.

"So, John, you weren't really around when Genie was a kid?" Leo continued his line of questions, inquiries she hadn't thought to ask them before.

"Unfortunately, I wasn't," John said, sounding genuinely remorseful.

"So Scott told you all about what a terrible mother I was? Is that what you are getting at?" Kitty growled. "That's about right. He never could take responsibility for *his* actions. Everything bad that ever happened between them was *my fault*."

"Why would you say that, Mrs. Manos?" Leo asked.

"I didn't say nothing. I was a damned good mom to Genie. I worked my fingers to the bone making sure she had food and clothing." She was gripping John's hands so hard that her nails were digging into the poor man's skin. "Genie wasn't the easiest kid and we definitely had some hard days, but for Scott to go around spitting lies—"

"Ma'am, I haven't said that Scott told me anything about your parenting or your relationship with your daughter. However, your reaction to my questions has me concerned. I feel as if there are some things that maybe you haven't been telling me, or the other detectives on my team, about Genie."

Kitty's mouth dropped open. "How *dare* you."

John stepped forward. "Genie and Kitty were like every mother and daughter. They had good times and bad. Lately, things had been better. Genie needed us, and we were there for her."

"I have no doubt about your helping Genie," Leo countered. "What I am wondering is if you and your wife knew things about Genie that you haven't yet disclosed?"

"Like what? We've told you everything you've needed to know," Kitty growled.

Aspen could tell that Leo had struck a nerve. "That I've *needed to know*?" he repeated. "Mr. and Mrs. Manos, did Genie have a drug problem?"

Kitty jerked toward him, but Leo didn't budge. Aspen took a step back and out of the woman's charge. "My daughter's life doesn't need to be investigated. All you need to worry about is finding her." She turned to Aspen, and her eyes were tight slits that made her appear nearly snakelike. "If anyone's behaviors and choices need to be looked into deeper, it is yours. We heard whispers about what happened at your camp last night. From the sounds of things, Aspen, we may well have made a mistake in hiring your group. As of this moment, you are fired."

Chapter Eighteen

Aspen's color faded from her cheeks as Leo moved closer to her in case her knees gave out and he had to catch her before she fell.

"I…" Aspen stammered, obviously taken by surprise. "*We*… *My team* has barely gotten started out here." She swallowed, hard.

"You have no right to take your anger out on Aspen and Chad," Leo said, trying to defend her. She was right. They had barely started and if they went back now he would be on his own…and she would be gone from his life forever.

"I'm not firing Chad," Kitty countered. "I'm only firing *her*. She clearly isn't capable. We heard she wasn't even on her boat yesterday. How are they supposed to work as a team if they don't even act like one?"

A sense of relief filled him. As angry as Kitty was, at least she didn't seem to know anything about their moment in the woods. If she had, he would be facing all kinds of inquiries at work. This mother was out for blood, and she was going to take out anyone who got in her way—friend or foe.

"If you fire me," Aspen said, sounding as though she had regained some amount of her resolve, "then Chad and our equipment will be leaving with me. Our fees for this week will still need to be paid."

John put his hand on Kitty's arm. "Look, we are already elbows deep in this. You're upset and we can talk about that when we get back to our condo, but for right now let's just let these good people get back to their job. They are our best chance of getting our Genie back."

He felt the pressure of their hate. Even though they had relatively little information or answers, he could tell that this case could easily become one that would haunt him for the rest of his career—whether or not Genie was located. If she wasn't, there would be all kinds of lawsuits from this family.

From here on out, he would have to tread carefully. Though they needed him, they weren't on the same side, especially given the fact that they were willing to turn on the people they themselves had hired after they thought his team wasn't doing their due diligence. No level of professional performance would assuage the terror and pain this family was feeling.

His heart went out to them. He felt for them, he really did, but he wished they could all be on the same page and working as a cohesive team instead of Kitty marking anyone who hadn't found her daughter as an enemy.

"Mrs. Manos," Leo said, lowering his voice and trying to sound as calm and soothing as possible, "Scott did tell me that you had a video that Genie sent to you. Apparently, it was a video of her and Scott fighting. You used it in order to help Genie press charges against Scott. Do you still have that video?"

"You better goddamn believe it," Kitty snarled.

"Would you mind sharing that video with me?"

"Don't you already have it? I used it to press the charges. Isn't it somewhere in your system or something?" Kitty flipped her hand around like his request was ridiculous and a nuisance.

It was strange, and he wasn't sure if he'd heard her quite right, but he could have sworn she had just said *she* pressed the charges. Regardless, he had bigger fish to fry.

"Ma'am, those charges were not in this county. As such, they are not easily available to my team," he said, though it wasn't entirely true. It was easy enough to make a call to Gallatin County where the fight had taken place and gain access to the video and PFMA report.

"It would help both of our teams if you would provide us with that video and any others that Genie may have shared with you, at least those that could pertain to this case and her husband," Aspen said, backing him up. "If something unfortunate has happened to your daughter, it could help us to understand what took place and perhaps make it easier for us to locate her…" She paused like she had almost slipped and said remains, but he was glad she stopped.

Kitty was enraged enough as it was. He didn't want to have the discussion about the possibility and likelihood of Genie being dead.

John nodded. "We will go through our information tonight after we talk to our lawyer."

Oh...damn. He had known that was coming; he just didn't know the attorney was going to roll into this so fast.

"I think that it understandable," he said, wishing he could tell them his thoughts about working on the same team; but no matter how he tried, they would never be able to see past their pain. "I just want to remind you, this is not currently a criminal investigation of any kind. However, in the future if we locate her remains, we may need to treat this case as such. Due to this, there are going to be elements of this case that we cannot disclose until we have completed our work."

"Just like I thought. You *are* hiding things from me," Kitty countered, stabbing her hand in his direction and looking toward John like he was the one on trial. "I told you, John. I freaking told you that these guys are only about themselves. They don't care about our Genie. They only care about covering their own butts. They are all in this together. They are covering something up."

"Ma'am," Leo said, trying to calm her, "I can assure you that we are not hiding anything that you need to know to find your daughter. We will tell you what we can, but we must be careful with any information that we disseminate. It could be detrimental to our case and our locating your daughter."

Kitty snarled at him. "Don't pretend you care about my daughter. All you care about is your stupid good ole boys club. I bet you're friends with Scott. I bet he is paying you off. I bet this is just some small-town conspiracy you have going on…and my daughter is the victim."

Aspen sucked in a breath like she was going to speak and once again try to come to his rescue, but he gently touched her arm with the back of his fingers to stop her. She didn't need to get in any deeper with her clients.

"Ma'am, you are clearly getting out of control here. I'm sorry that you feel as you do toward my team and myself. However, once again, I can assure you that we are doing everything in our power to find and bring your daughter back home."

"I'll show you out of control," Kitty said, raising her hand as she moved to strike.

John threw his arms around her body and pulled her back. "We will be in touch."

They watched as John led Kitty toward their high-end SUV. He pushed her into the passenger seat. Kitty dropped her head into her hands, and her back began to shake with sobs.

His heart shattered as he watched the mother dissolve before him.

These were the moments that had made him into the hardened man, the man who couldn't sleep out of the fear that nightmares would flood his mind— nightmares filled with moments of watching mothers mourn.

THEY WATCHED AS John started the car and took off, leaving a cloud of dust in his wake. Aspen didn't know how Leo had managed to maintain his composure. She was enraged, and most of Kitty's tirade hadn't been directed at her. If anything, she had been nothing more than collateral damage.

"Thank you, Leo," she said.

"For what?" he asked, taking out his phone and looking at it.

"For saving my job," she said, surprised that he even had to ask. "If it wasn't for you, I'd be on the next plane back with Chad."

Leo threw his head back slightly as he sighed. "Oh, yeah… *Chad.*"

Her gut ached.

"Let's rip off the Band-Aid," he said, stuffing his phone in his pocket.

As they walked by Leo's pickup, he poked his head into the truck where Chewy was kenneled. The dog wagged his tail, but didn't even bother to get up as they peeked in on him.

"At least one of us is having a good day," he said with a chuckle.

She didn't know how to respond. Her instinct was to try to make things better and fix the situation, but there was no fixing or making things better. There was only moving forward through the muck and hoping to eventually make it out to the other side—the side that held some much-needed answers.

Chad had the window down and was looking smug as they approached the pickup.

"Hey, man," Leo said, approaching the vehicle. "How's it going?"

Chad chuckled. "You know I hate to say I enjoyed that, but I thoroughly enjoyed watching that lady own your ass. I had five bucks on her throwing hands."

"I wasn't sure she wasn't. It was a good thing that John was there to keep her under some manner of control."

Chad nodded. "No kidding. It's one thing for me to kick your ass, and it's another for you to get your butt handed to you by a fiftysomething mom."

"Oh, you kicked my butt? Is that how we are spinning this story?" Leo asked, an edge of playfulness in his tone.

"The way I see it. You guys need me." Chad placed his phone on the console. "*You* need me, Aspen."

"Chad," she said, "I need to know that you can be trusted to keep quiet about what you saw last night. If not, everyone involved in this search could be in deep trouble. As you may have heard, they have hired lawyers. It's only a matter of time until we are all dragged into court."

"Then we definitely need to find Genie," Chad said, not really answering. "I hate court dates, and there is no way I'm traveling back to this state just to sit in front of a judge."

"I agree. But again, Chad, can we trust you?" she pressed.

"If I get put on the witness stand, I'm not going to cover or lie for you. However," Chad said looking between them, "as long as you two knock it off and keep it in your pants, we can leave what happened in the woods out there."

"Ass kickings included?" Leo asked, motioning his chin toward Chad's eye.

"I still stand by the fact that I kicked your ass," Chad said, chuckling. "And hey, for what it's worth, I was kind of acting like a jerk. I really shouldn't drink…and hey, I'm sorry about the thing with the gun."

"So that's what's really behind this? You moved that gun?" Aspen asked, trying not to sound too accusatorial.

"I didn't mean to. I just wanted to take a look at it and I thought I put it back in the right spot, but I was in a hurry after I ran into you guys out in the woods," Chad said, a flash of anger in his eyes.

"Well, then, it looks like we all made our share of mistakes last night," Leo said. "I appreciate you owning up to what happened—answers a lot of questions."

"Yeah," Chad said with a slight nod. "Let's just leave it all out there."

She tried not to take Leo's comment to heart and instead remain objective. *They* had made a misstep in falling into each other's arms and Chad had been well…*Chad*. She still thought he was a jerk, but at least he was a jerk who saw that by digging in the mud, they were all going to get dirty.

Chapter Nineteen

After running Chewy back to his house, Leo sat in the main conference room at the search and rescue warehouse. The room was normally set aside for debriefings, planning upcoming training sessions and, when time allowed, working out the details of missions. He'd spent so much time in this room that in many ways it felt like home. This was one of the few places on the planet where everything was secure and where he could trust all those around him. In every other facet of his life, it felt like people were pandering or posing, whatever it took to get what they wanted from him.

Here, in this place, he was allowed the freedom to make the decisions he thought best that would bring them success in bringing people home. Generally there were no politics or favors to navigate, only life and death. He'd take that kind of authenticity every day.

Maybe that was why he felt so out of place in this room today, or it could have been the fact that he was once again face-to-face with the one woman he couldn't stop thinking about.

Aspen was hovering over the PFMA report that he'd pulled from Gallatin County while they waited for both the county and Kitty to send their copies of the videos. While he assumed they would be exactly the same footage, with the way things were going in this case, it wouldn't hurt for him to take a look and make sure. In fact, moving forward he would be looking more deeply into everything involving this case.

"Aspen, are you working for Life Savers full-time?" he asked, curious about how she had found herself in this backcountry town in the belly of Montana.

She looked up from the report. "I am."

"Do you own the organization?"

She shook her head. "I am just the coordinator. The group has been around for forty years and it is still held by the family who started it, though they don't take a very active role in its management anymore. The younger generation doesn't hold a great deal of interest."

"That's interesting. I would think that adventurers and rescuers would raise future generations of the same."

The corners of her mouth quirked up. "So, you think that people are born into their roles and personalities?"

"I think free will always plays a factor, but take me for example. My parents were always out in the woods of Montana. I couldn't have been happy cooped up in a cubicle every day of my life."

"Don't you though, you know, working as a detective?" she asked, sounding genuinely curious.

"I spend far more time than I would like, but I do enjoy my job." He picked up a wayward pen on the table and turned it in his fingers. "Though, I have to admit I miss my work on patrol. We were always doing something, even when we weren't busy we were busy."

"You're not busy as a detective?"

"Oh, that's not it at all," he said, taken slightly aback. "I'm busier than I've ever been. I feel like there's never enough time in the day. And most of the time, just like this case with the Manoses, I feel like I'm letting people down."

Her features softened as she glanced over at him. "You're not letting them down."

"You know that I am. Sure, I may not be able to control things, but you and I are the ones who have the most pivotal roles." He paused, suddenly wondering if he shouldn't have said what was on his mind. If she didn't feel guilty, then he shouldn't give her that weight to bear.

"Just because we haven't found her, it doesn't mean that we won't."

Chad and Cindy walked into the meeting area.

"Hey, guys," Aspen said, turning to them. "I'm glad to see you made it."

Cindy had a wide smile. "Actually, I've had my hands full this morning. While you guys were working on the press and getting things handled on your end, I went to check on Malice."

"He still doing okay?" Leo asked.

Cindy pulled out her phone. "Actually, we missed some things when we first looked over that poor pup."

"Did he have gun residue on his paws?" Leo asked, trying to make things light.

Cindy let out a wry laugh. "Real funny," she said, putting her phone on the table in front of him. "Did you know that the dog was microchipped?"

He pulled her phone closer and looked at a picture taken a year or so before of the German shepherd, who was lying on the floor. He looked to be heavier and in better body condition. "What am I looking at here, Cindy?"

Cindy's smile grew impossibly wider. "Well, I found out that the dog actually doesn't belong to Genie. The registered owner is Jamie Offerman."

"Are you sure?" he asked.

Cindy zoomed out on the picture. Standing beside the dog was Jamie, the high school secretary he had originally spoken to when Genie had disappeared.

Jamie hadn't mentioned anything about the dog being legally hers; or that she had even known Genie. Even if Genie had adopted the dog from the local shelter, there was no way that Jamie wouldn't have known the dog when she had seen it. Or had she never seen the dog and Genie? If he remembered correctly, Genie had been reported missing before Jamie had even arrived at the beach and a woman in her thirties had called in the suspicious activity. She had only acted as the mouthpiece.

He talked to Jamie often. She had always been more than forthcoming with information when it involved one of the students at the local high school. If she had any sort of connection to Genie and the missing dog, she would have said something to him. At least, he believed she would have.

Yet, it seemed as he dug further into each of his questions in reference to this disappearance, he kept finding that instead of getting answers, he only found himself drowning in more questions.

There were so many facets to this case, each bringing a new perspective. It was almost overwhelming.

"Where did you get this picture of Jamie with the dog?" he asked, looking up at Cindy and Chad.

"Social media. That pic was from last summer." Cindy looked over at Chad. "He messaged her."

Leo wasn't sure that he liked that they were acting like the detectives on the case, but he appreciated that they were showing gumption and getting answers. "And? Did Jamie respond?"

Chad smiled. "She did. I liked the picture, and we got to talking about her and the dog. She said she didn't have it anymore—got lost. She put out flyers around town, but never got anywhere with the search."

"This town isn't that big. If she put word out on social media that a dog was missing, the animal would have been back the same day," Leo said. "I've seen it a million times on there. She's lying to you." His stomach sank.

"That's what I thought, too," Chad said. "It's why we came to talk to you, right away."

"Thanks," he said, still not trusting that Chad had anything but his own best interests in mind. "Did you talk to Jamie about anything else?"

"She hinted at the fact that she hasn't been out on a date in a long time. I think if you need me to I could pry more information from her."

Aspen sent him a look like she thought it wasn't the worst idea that Chad had ever had, but Leo wasn't sure he was on board with the idea. He didn't like things to be out of his control when it came to investigations, and they were already on unsteady ground.

"I will keep that offer in mind. We will see if we need to take things in that direction. As it stands, I'm going to need to give her a call and ask her some questions regarding the dog and her role in everything."

Chad frowned. "Don't you think that if you do, you'll be tipping your hand too soon?"

He gritted his teeth. Of course, Chad thought he knew more about his job than he did. As much as he wanted to bite, he resisted the urge. They were on civil terms, and it was best to keep things that way.

"I'll let you know if I learn anything of value." He turned to Aspen. "In the meantime, you and I can run over to the high school where Jamie works—she should be in the office today. Gallatin County should have the reports and videos to us in the next hour or so, as long as they aren't too busy. Is there anything else you'd like for us to do, Cindy?" Leo asked.

"Sounds like you have everything under control," she said.

He flipped the pen in his fingers and then set it down on the table like he was marking her spot. "You guys need to look over the water flows. I'm thinking we need to go down the river again."

Cindy gave him a brief nod. "Do you mind helping, Chad?"

He nodded, but there was something in the way he moved toward Cindy that raised a flag with him. There was a familiarity between them that hadn't been there before. He'd like to have assumed it was because of their time on the boat that had bonded them, but something told him there was more to their friendship.

If Chad started to date Cindy, he would laugh his ass off.

Then again, maybe that was part of the reason he had been so suddenly understanding and apologetic about their fight.

It didn't take long for him and Aspen to make their way over to the local high school, home of the Eagles. The place was adorned with blue and gold, and the parking lot was littered with spent soda cans and discarded homework. There were a few cars in the parking lot, and until now he had forgotten that school had gotten out for the summer holiday last week.

Hopefully Jamie was still working or it would be a little tougher to track her down.

Parking near the front entrance, in what was normally the loop reserved for the buses, he and Aspen got out and made their way up to the front double doors. The entrance was locked, so he pressed the little silver button attached to the intercom by the door.

"Hello?" he asked, hoping there was someone other than a janitor there to answer him.

"Yes?" a woman answered.

"We are here looking for Jamie Offerman. She is a friend of mine. Is she working today or is she off for the holidays?" he asked.

"Leo? You should have told me you were coming," the woman said excitedly. "I'm in the office wrapping things up. Come on in."

The door buzzed as it opened.

"Jamie can come on a little strong," he said quietly to Aspen as they made their way inside. Their footfalls echoed on the hard tile floor as they made their way toward the main office at the heart of the building.

"What does that mean?" she asked.

"You'll see," he said, winking at her.

Jamie was standing outside the door of the glass-walled office and was waving wildly as he and Aspen approached. He wasn't sure, but he could have sworn that Jamie's smile flickered when she spotted Aspen, but she quickly looked away from her and stared directly at him.

"Jamie." He said her name jovially. "Nice to see you again."

Her smile widened, and a little color rose in her cheeks. She looked like she had been spending time out in the sun and her skin was far more tanned than when he'd seen her a few weeks ago.

"Leo," she said, coming up to him and giving him a little hug and a quick, almost territorial kiss to his cheek. "I'm so glad to see you. I hate when school gets out. I don't get to talk to you as much." Finally, she let go of him and deigned to finally speak to Aspen. "Hi."

Leo turned to Aspen and sent her a guilty, I-told-you-so smile. "Jamie, this is my friend Aspen from Minnesota who works with the Life Savers group. She's helping us look for Genie. You might have seen her the day Genie went missing."

"Oh, yeah." The ice in Jamie's demeanor melted, and she stuck her hand out to Aspen. "Hey, it's nice to meet you—officially. Chad told me a lot about your organization."

"He did? That's great. I'm proud of the work we do." Aspen gave her hand a quick shake and Jamie turned away. "Sounds like you are busy around here, too."

"Oh, yeah, I've had my work cut out for me ever since the kids were let out of school for the break. I'm playing catch up on all the work and duties that get overlooked when I have kids streaming in and out of my office." Jamie chattered away as she led them into her area. "Though, I have to admit I miss all the sounds of the kids. When they are here, I get to listen in on all the coming and goings. It's awful quiet when they aren't here."

Her office was littered with stacks of papers, and the walls were adorned with awards and accolades the school had received over the years. He'd been in this office a number of times, but he'd never really noticed the framed certificates before. It was nice to see the principal and staff were getting recognized for the work they did for the community and the children and families who resided here.

He had gone to this school when he'd been a kid, but it had changed so much in the last twenty years that it was nearly unrecognizable. The only things that hadn't really changed was the constant scent of adolescents and the heavy mask of industrial cleaners they used to try to disinfect the petri dish that was a school.

He missed the days of fall football and the sounds of the crowds in the stands, cheering as he ran the ball. Aspen would have been one hell of a cheerleader, the little skirt riding up as she jumped on the track. Then again, she was far too serious to be the kind to bounce around and do flips. If he had to guess, she was probably more of a basketball player. She was tall enough and in shape, the kind of body that came with years of exercise.

Jamie was still talking, but it took him a moment to realize that she was asking him a question.

"Excuse me?" he asked, trying to act like he had just managed to miss what she'd said instead of being caught completely ignoring her.

"I was just asking what brought you to me today," Jamie said, touching him gently on the arm. "Do you need a drink? To sit down? I bet you're exhausted after all the things I've heard you've been doing lately."

"Actually, I'm here to ask you about a dog."

Jamie tilted her head. "What dog?"

"We located a German shepherd recently," he said, not adding any unnecessary details. "It was found that the dog was registered to you when he was scanned for a microchip."

Jamie grasped her hands in front of her body as she sighed.

"By chance," he continued, as he tried to make heads or tails of her body language, "did you have a German shepherd who got lost? Or maybe you gave him up for adoption?"

She shook her head. "Malice wasn't my dog."

"So, you do know what dog I'm talking about?" he asked.

She nodded, finally looking up. "Yes, I bought him for my daughter. She needed a pet to help her with her mental health."

That explained why the dog may have been registered under her name, but it still didn't give him the answers he so desperately needed. "I didn't know you had children, Jamie."

"Yes, two. I have Edith and Mary. Mary is twenty-three and she lives in San Diego with her longtime boyfriend, and Edith just turned nineteen. She graduated from here last year and…well, she is taking a gap year and staying with friends for the time being. The dog was hers."

"Did Edith give the dog up for adoption?" he asked.

"The last I knew, she still had the dog, but I guess she must have dumped him—or gave him to a friend."

She shook her head, but quickly turned away and hid her face. "Where did you find him?"

"We found him by the river. He wasn't in good condition. He is with the veterinarian now, recovering."

"I would be happy to cover the costs. Do you have the vet's number? I'll call them right away."

Aspen gave him a look of surprise. "Mrs. Offerman, we believe this dog may have been the dog that Genie had with her when she disappeared."

Jamie's mouth dropped open with shock. "What? No."

"Do you know how your dog, or your daughter's dog, would have fallen into Genie's custody?" Leo asked. "Did Genie and Edith know one another?"

Jamie ran her hand over her face, pinching the bridge of her nose. "I don't know if they were friends, exactly. I do know they have been in the past, but lately they've been having some run-ins. She and Genie got into a pretty big tussle out on my front lawn. I pulled them apart and Edith turned on me. That was the last day I saw Edith or Malice—that was the day my daughter wrote me off as her mother."

Chapter Twenty

Though they had some direction to dig deeper when it came to the dog, Aspen wasn't entirely sure that this was the way they needed to push their search. At least, not for her and Chad. It was interesting and there was certainly a great deal of drama at every turn, and everyone had their stories, but she couldn't help feeling like they were falling further and further behind in their search for Genie.

The truck came to a stop at the light as they headed back toward the warehouse.

"Leo," she said, "I know you probably want to do more work on the case, running down leads and everything. I understand that, but I feel like I need to get back out to the river and get my boots dirty."

Leo looked down at the clock on the dashboard. "I hear you," he said, "but if we went out right now, we'd be spending another night out in the woods, and I think we both know how that turned out last time." He sent her an endearing smile.

She wanted to tell him that their night out hadn't been so bad, that was if it had just remained their little secret. Yet, he was right. She wasn't sure that she wanted to be put in a similar situation, surrounded by people at the very least, again.

On the other hand, she had spent quite a bit of time alone with him today, and she hadn't been overtaken by lust or want and done anything that went against the agreement they had made with one another.

He reached over and pushed a button on the radio, switching the station to hard rock. Godsmack was playing, and he started to dip his head in beat with the music. "I've seen these guys three times in concert. Sully is the man."

She had never been huge on hard rock, but good music was good music and Godsmack had never disappointed.

"Is Chewy a fan, too?" she giggled.

"Any dog of mine has to love the finer things in life," he said, sending her a brilliant smile that made her think of his face when she had stepped out from behind the tree last night. That look, that *smile*…it could make her forget her own name.

He was so incredibly handsome.

"Finer things, eh?" she teased, motioning toward the fast-food wrapper that was wadded up and tossed on the floorboard near her feet.

"You can't bag on the double Quarter Pounder with cheese. Like they said in *Pulp Fiction*, they 'are the cornerstone of any nutritious breakfast.'"

There was that smile again, the one that made her body tighten and ache.

"If you are going to pull one-liners from that movie

about burgers, I'm shocked you didn't give me the name of it in French."

"Oh, you mean because they use the metric system? They call it the Royale with cheese."

She laughed, sticking out her tongue at him. "Oh, you know-it-all."

"Don't hate, now," he said, laughing. "You had to have guessed I'm a Tarantino fan."

"What?" She feigned shock that this total type A with a proven hero complex would like action flicks with high danger and even higher body counts. "I really thought you'd be more of a ballet fan."

He gave her a look like he was trying to decide if she was serious or just playing with him, and the way he questioned it made her like him a little more. She liked that he was paying attention, and that he looked deeper into what people were saying...and more at how they said it. So much could be gleaned from body language—far more honesty was in a person's actions.

She had needed to find this...*softness* in him. He was such a cowboy, strong and austere, that he was hard to read sometimes. More, he had almost seemed to have perfected the art of masking his emotions. For him to open up and laugh with her meant something. Even Smash had told her that he was the kind who was all business all the time.

It made her smile to think that even after they had made a mistake together, that there was still something there—even if it was a spark that they couldn't capture and use to reignite the flames.

TRUTH BE TOLD, he had really been enjoying having a buddy with him in his mobile office, otherwise known as his pickup, and it surprised him. He spent so many hours alone in this damned thing that had it been anyone but Aspen, he wasn't sure that he would have liked the company. He liked having his own private space where he could work and take lunch, a place away from what felt like a rotating door in his office.

No matter what he was doing, it always felt like he couldn't finish one task without being barraged by a hundred others. Even if he worked all day every day, he wasn't idealistic enough to think he would even make a dent in the workload in the detectives' department.

Aspen was humming as he glanced over at her, and her blond hair was flashing almost gold in the sun. For the first time since he'd met her, she truly seemed happy. Well, except for the brief moment together last night. Damn, she had been ready. And oh…the way she had tasted.

He had to shift in his seat in order to hide what his thoughts were doing to him.

Leo's phone rang and he was grateful as he answered. "Hello?"

The call came on over Bluetooth, connecting to the radio. "Hey, Detective West," a man said. The ID came up as Madison County—it was the 911 dispatch. "We just received a report about a piece of clothing that matches the description of those that your missing girl was wearing. Do you want to take the call or would you rather we sent it out to one of your deputies?"

Leo pulled over to the side of the road. "What was found? Who found it?"

There was the clicking of keys as the man must have been typing. "A fisherman reported finding a pair of hot pink bikini bottoms, size small."

"A fisherman? Did you catch his name?" he asked, thinking about his recent development with Jamie and Edith.

"Some guy named Jordan Vedere."

The name didn't ring a bell. So either the guy was a tourist, which were all-too common during the ski season and then the fly-fishing season, which co-incided with bug hatches, or he wasn't a frequent flyer with the department. Either way, he was glad it wasn't someone who they had been looking into regarding their case. He was getting tired of being taken by surprise.

"Would you like me to put it out on the board?" the man asked.

"I got it. Thanks, dispatch." Leo tapped his fingers on the wheel. "Would you please send me the pin for the coordinates where the item was located?"

"You got it." There was a pause and the clicking of keys. "I sent it straight to your phone. Do you need anything else from me?"

"Nah, but thank you, dispatch."

"Good luck. Stay safe." The dispatcher hung up.

He clicked on his phone and stared at the GPS coordinates. He knew the place, but it hadn't been somewhere he'd worked in a few years, so he couldn't recall exactly how to get to the area. He moved the map around, looking for an area where they could park and then hike.

"Do you recognize where the bottoms were found?" Aspen asked.

"Looks like they were a couple miles down from where we took out." He zoomed in on the coordinates. "From the map, it appears as though there is an inlet right after the pin." Leo turned the truck around and started to drive in the direction of the river. He called Cindy as he drove.

"Hello?" Cindy answered.

"We're not going to be back to the warehouse," he said. "We just got a call from dispatch, and it sounds like a guy possibly just located half of Genie's swimsuit."

"Half?" Cindy asked.

"Yeah." He tried not to sound too excited about this newest potential break in their case.

"But no body?" she asked.

"So far, doesn't sound like it. Only thing I know is that it was just the bottoms of her swimsuit near a river inlet not far from where we had been searching."

"Interesting," Cindy said. "Do you need me down there? What about the rest of the team? Want me to make some calls?"

SAR members didn't normally help with evidence recovery; the gun had been an outlier due to the location and his being there, so her offer was more of a platitude than a real option. Nonetheless, he appreciated it. He really did have a great team.

"Thanks, but I want you guys to get the next mission together. I'm thinking we run the river from the point we left off."

"I think that's cool," Cindy said, sounding hesitant, "however, the water has come up four inches today and the CFS is running hot."

The cubic feet per second—CFS—was a factor that would dictate if they could even get on the water or if their getting back out there would have to wait until the river stopped surging once again.

"Crap," he said. "Well, you make the determination whether or not we can hit it again."

"Will do. I'll get more information about what the temps are supposed to be tomorrow morning." Cindy paused for a brief second. "If you want to try it, we may be able to go out, but it's going to have to be as soon as the sun rises and it's cool. We'd have to be off well in advance of noon. We don't want to get put into a hairy situation."

The flows had already been running pretty fast. When this happened, the strainers became even more dangerous and difficult to navigate. Often, trees would be ripped out of the banks and pulled downstream, making impassible blockades in the river that just waited for unwary boaters.

If a team got stuck in one of those dam-like structures, the boats would get torn up and capsize. Once that happened, which could take just a matter of seconds, the people on board would get sucked under by the fast-moving water, or swept against and hooked up on broken limbs and branches. Once, when the water subsided and the CFS went back to normal, he had been called out for a body that had been located hanging three feet off the top of the water.

The person who had found the remains had assumed the person had tried to hang themselves. When he arrived, the man was wearing only a T-shirt, which was pulled up high over his head, his bloated body keeping him in place as the water pounded against his fish-nibbled legs.

At first glance, thanks to the odd placement of the sun-bleached shirt, it did look like the man had somehow strangled himself. However, further investigation had revealed that the man had been involved in a boating accident early in the summer—he had gone under and never resurfaced. Likely, close to the time he sank, he'd gotten wrapped up in the downfall and he'd never come back out.

For being out in the elements as long as he had, his body had actually been in pretty good condition; it had been an unusually cold spring and summer.

"You okay?" Aspen asked, motioning toward Cindy's name on the truck's screen.

He gave her a curt nod. "All right, Cindy, you plan on things for tomorrow. Let's just keep our fingers crossed that the river doesn't blow out while we get things together." He hung up and looked over at Aspen. If the river was out, then Kitty Manos was going to go absolutely bonkers on them—none more so than Aspen.

If they didn't get some kind of answers soon, Aspen would most definitely be going home.

Chapter Twenty-One

The guy who had called in the bikini was sitting on the bank of the river, eating a sandwich that looked like it came from the local diner. As they approached the guy didn't seem to notice them, and as Leo neared, he spotted the little earbuds stuffed in the guy's ears.

He'd never understand why someone would want to come out to the middle of nature and then block out the sounds. He found the sounds of the birds calling and the water rushing incredibly calming and peaceful, though he was rarely alone out here anymore. All his time was spent at work, training or working with SAR.

If anything, he envied the guy that he even got the chance to check out from the realities of life—even if he squandered it in a way.

The guy jumped as they approached from behind and Leo tapped him on the shoulder.

If they had been a bear or other predatory animal, the guy would have been as good as dead. He took a little bit of guilty pleasure in the realization, though he knew he shouldn't have.

"How's it going?" he asked.

"Hey." The man pulled his earbuds out and put them away in a little white case, then looked up at him. "You a game warden?" he asked, looking at Leo for some kind of identifying markers and then to Aspen.

She was wearing a thin jacket with the Life Savers logo embroidered on the chest.

"No," Leo said. "I'm Detective West from the Madison County Sheriff's Office. We received a call that someone out here had found an item of interest. Are you Jordan Vedere?"

Jordan stood up and brushed the sandwich crumbs off his waders—waders that looked nearly brand-new and that Leo knew cost at least five hundred bucks at the local fly shop. "Yeah, that's me." He didn't stick out his hand, instead he stuck his thumbs into the straps of his waders and puffed his chest out.

"Catch any today?" he asked, trying to make nice.

Jordan nodded and stepped over toward where his clean-handled Winston sat haphazardly on the rocks. The sight of the very expensive, brand-new rod sitting so unloved and uncared for made Leo cringe.

The man grabbed ahold of a seven-inch rainbow trout, which had started to dry out and stiffen in the sun. "Got this hog." He smiled proudly.

There was no way Vedere was from around here. No one around here kept their catch. It was all catch and release because it was part of being a good sportsman and conservationist, and most people couldn't stand the muddy and fishy flavor—not that this fish looked remotely edible. By the time he got it home and out of the sun, it would likely smell to high heaven.

Ah, tourists.

"Nice job," Aspen said, but Leo could hear the tone in her voice, which told him that she was holding back a judgmental laugh.

He was glad that she saw Jordan for who he really was—someone who didn't understand the beauty of the experience and cared more about the pomp and accessories than the actual sport.

Regardless, he was glad the guy had been out here. Well, *maybe*…that was, if the bikini was actually tied to their case.

"So, can you show us to the area in which you found the item?" he asked.

"Yeah, no problem," Jordan said. His boots slipped on the wet rocks as they made their way farther down river, near the inlet.

There, near the edge of the water, was a hot pink woman's bikini bottom. It looked as though it was wrapped around a large stick.

"There you go." Jordan pointed in the direction. "You guys mind if I get back to fishing? I've been waiting for you for a bit. Need to get more on the bank, ya know?" He sounded genuinely excited.

"Did you disturb the suit at all?" Leo asked, before allowing the man to leave.

Jordan shook his head.

"Perfect. I have your information from dispatch. If I have any questions, would it be all right if I call?"

"Yeah, whatever you need is fine."

"Good luck," Aspen said, but there was a huge smile on her face.

The guy might catch another fish, but he wasn't going to catch anything of value so far away from a good food source. Regardless, he was allowed his fun.

"Thank you for calling in your find," Leo said.

The man waved, turning away from them and carefully picking his way down the riverbank until he wound around the bend and out of view.

"You think those are hers?" Aspen turned to him and asked.

"I'd say the odds are pretty good." He took out his phone and snapped a few pictures of the item as they approached.

At first glance, he'd thought the bikini bottom was merely wrapped on the stick, but now as he looked closer it appeared as though the stick had ripped into the fabric and was caught. The branch was still covered in bark, but some of it had been ripped away where it looked like the fabric had rubbed hard against it…probably due to the weight of the person who had been wearing them compounded by the inertia of the water.

"Oh," Aspen said.

"You know what this likely means…finding this here and presenting like this?" He paused. "Our girl was in the river and at some point, she was probably caught on a downed tree and pushed by the current. She must be out here in the river or on a riverbank somewhere if she broke loose from that tree—but now, between the dog's location and this, I think it is safe to assume she is dead."

Aspen ran her hands over her face like she wasn't exactly surprised by the news but was disappointed. "Kitty and John aren't going to take this news well."

He shook his head. "No, no they aren't."

They stood staring at the pink bikini bottom. Leo moved around it, snapping a few more pictures of the item in situ. He squatted, taking a few more pictures close up, making sure to get the tag on the suit, the spot where the limb pierced the fabric and the way the fabric seemed stretched and marred by the bark and pressure. He was positive that Genie had been wearing these when they had caught on a limb. With the increase in the CFS, maybe it had created enough pressure to pull her body free of her piece of clothing. He'd seen this kind of thing before and it never led to a happy ending.

Without a doubt, they were working on body recovery as there was no longer any residual hope of a rescue. He was saddened, but at the same time he was glad they were getting some answers for the family. Their daughter could likely be presumed dead. As such, they could move forward with all the legal work that came with his finding.

He would have to call Scott.

This entire situation was a tough one, but it was hardly the first time he had witnessed a family at odds during an investigation. More times than not, families wanted to point fingers and blame everyone around them when it came to the death of someone they loved—especially when that person was young.

For all involved, he hoped that if they found Genie's body it would come to light that this was nothing more than a tragic accident. If not, Scott and his in-laws would probably sink deeper into their war with each other and with him and the folks he worked with.

He would have to call the family later, but first he wanted to get his ducks in a row. He took a series of notes about the bottoms and his collection methods before he stuffed his phone into his pocket and, putting down his backpack, he reached inside and took out his evidence collection kit. He slipped on a pair of nitrile gloves and removed a plastic bag that would be large enough to fit the section of the broken branch as well as the bottoms. If he had to guess, his tech would likely be able to pull more trace evidence to support his belief that these had been worn by Genie. It wouldn't even surprise him if they found skin cells buried under the rough bark.

"Do you want to run this over to the crime lab and then we can come back and continue our search?" Aspen asked.

He sighed. It was an option, but now that they were gaining ground and he felt like he was approaching real answers, he didn't want to leave. "Let's work the area until dark. We'll search the bank for the next mile or so downstream. I think that this should be the point where we work from, as this is a good indicator that she was here. Let's treat this as her last known location."

She nodded. "Great idea." She smiled, her perfect teeth shining in the sun and pulling his thoughts from their somewhat macabre discovery and reminding him of how beautiful she was.

This was going to be a great day, he could feel it—the energy in the air was palpable and he wasn't sure if it was because of the thrill of gaining ground on their case or if it was that smile and the fact that he was working with the most beautiful woman he'd ever known. If pressed to answer, he would have had to admit it was likely a combination of both.

It would be a hell of a thing to be able to have her at his side all the time. They made a pretty great team. She was good at this line of work and she seemed to love it as much, if not more, than he did.

He gently put the evidence he'd collected into his backpack and then slipped it onto his back, and it reminded him of the misallocated gun. His stomach knotted. He hated what Chad had done.

Regardless, that wasn't happening again. It was critical that these bottoms never leave his personal gear. Though, he had doubted it was Aspen who had taken or moved the gun. Thinking about his faux pas and the gun gave him a headache.

He sighed.

"We will find her," Aspen said.

He nodded. "I hope so."

"Do you think this was an accidental drowning?" she asked, sounding genuinely curious.

"I want to say yes, but finding that gun registered to Scott is throwing me. I can't imagine why she would have been swimming with a gun. And if it hadn't been on her, there were no reports of her being there with another person…so how did it get out there by Malice? Ya know?" His face scrunched.

"I've been thinking about that, too." She nibbled on her lip like she was deep in thought. "I'm hoping we find her with a fanny pack on or a chest harness, or something."

He nodded. "That would be nice, but in the video she was only wearing the bikini. Though, that doesn't mean anything. She could have put something on after she played in the water with the dog." He started to pick his way down the riverbank, looking for anything else that might have been tied to their search.

"That's my hope." She moved a few feet to his right, searching the area not directly in his line of sight and expanding their coverage.

"Okay," he said, "let's say we are right and she was the one who had possession of the weapon. Why would it not still be tucked away on her person? Why would it have been found by the dog?"

"That is the part I can't make sense of."

They walked in silence as he pored over all the different possibilities and explanations, but nothing he came up with made logical sense. They just didn't have enough information.

They made their way down the bank, working the area until the sun started to slip behind the tops of the mountain. "Let's head back," he finally said, somewhat disappointed that they hadn't found more.

Aspen nodded and even though he could tell she

was physically tired, she looked as beautiful as ever thanks to her ruddy cheeks and sweaty brow. "I needed this."

They turned and started to work an area tucked farther away from the river in an effort to cover extra ground.

"What do you mean by that?" he asked.

She looked over at him and smiled. "I just meant it feels good to be putting my boots to the ground a little more. I like working the water, and I think this will help if we get the chance to hit the water again tomorrow. But you've been great in helping me to learn the terrain."

He was taken slightly aback by her compliment. "Where did that come from?" he asked.

"You know," she teased, "most people say thank you when they get a compliment."

He chuckled. "Yes… I mean *thank you.*"

She moved a little bit closer to him until the backs of their hands brushed against each other. The action made electrical sparks race up his arms and his heart sputter.

She had promised that she wasn't going to flirt with him or allow things to go the way they had last night, but as she touched him he found himself wishing that she would.

"You are seeming to like Montana," he said, trying not to delve down the path of questioning why she was touching him and if it was on purpose or inadvertent.

She couldn't have been doing it on accident, though.

They both were experts when it came to searches like this, and her being so close to him definitely broke the rules. Which meant she had to *want* to touch him.

He wasn't sure if he should make a move and slip his hand into hers. If he did, he also wasn't sure how she would respond. This, being around her and wanting her more, was driving him wild.

Maybe if they just had real, down and dirty sex, then maybe he could go back to focusing on their mission and not the fact that he wanted to rip her clothes off and pull her down on top of him. Yes, he could really go for that right now…on the riverbank as the water slipped by.

They were alone. The only other person out here was the fisherman, but he had to be at least a mile upstream…*if* he was even still out here. It was starting to get dark, which meant it was hard to see his knots or the flies on the water, so he had probably packed it in and was headed back to his car by now.

Really, except for the agreement they'd made to leave their relationship as just a friendship there was nothing else to stop them from taking things further.

Plus this time, there was no ethical conundrum as to whether or not they were on the clock. They had completed their search and were just heading back.

He gave a small laugh as he realized he was trying to talk himself into sex when really there was no need—he knew what he wanted. The only real question was whether or not she wanted him or if she was playing with his body and his heart.

He had to find out, but how?

As they moved up a hill, she was breathing hard. He let her walk slightly ahead of him so she could set the pace and, slightly selfishly, so he could stare at her ass. It was nearly in his face as she dug the toes of her boots into the hillside and climbed.

He loved the way her pants pulled against her muscular behind. She definitely hiked a lot back at home in Minnesota.

Minnesota. He'd never really hated a state before, and yet he found himself hating it like it was a person who had kicked his dog.

Cresting the top of the hill, he paused, not ready to give up or rush this private time together. He turned toward the river below, looking down on the bank where they had walked earlier.

As the sun set around them, the sky turned colors, the pink, purple and orange fingers reaching out overhead. The sunset reflected off the water, mirroring the grandeur of the snowy peaks of the mountains and the sky.

Aspen stepped beside him, slipping her hand in his without saying a word.

It was perfect—her hand in his, the sky, the river, the heat of her body pressing against his. He could have lived in this moment forever.

Chapter Twenty-Two

Aspen leaned against him on the overlook as they stared out at the sunset. She hadn't expected this moment, but she was grateful she had been given this chance to stand with him and share what was hands down the most breathtaking moment she'd ever experienced in nature.

It had to be a sign.

Leo ran his thumb over the back of her hand, and she gripped his tighter, hugging him in the only way she could think of to gently show him that she still wanted to be with him—even if she had said otherwise.

"Aspen." He whispered her name as though he was afraid that the sound of his voice would take something away from the moment.

"Mmm-hmm?"

"I hope you know how much I still want you," he said, turning to look at her.

His directness surprised her. She looked up into his brown eyes and found that they were reflecting the rainbow of colors cast by the setting sun. It felt as if she was looking into the eyes of some other-worldly god.

He was so incredibly handsome that her mouth watered and, for the first time, she wondered if she was pretty enough to be with him. Leo was the kind of man who could have anyone he wanted, and yet... here he was, choosing her.

She was the luckiest woman in the world.

She pulled his hand around her back and let go of his fingers. Reaching up, she ran her fingers through his damp hair. "You're sweaty," she said, her voice soft and supplicating.

"Mmm-hmm," he said, staring down at her lips. He pulled her hard against his body. "Do you have any idea how beautiful you are?" he asked, finally looking up from her lips and their eyes locked.

She smiled.

"From the first time I saw you—"

"You mean when you hated me?" she interrupted playfully.

"I didn't hate you. I've never hated you."

"You didn't seem to like me when Cindy introduced us."

"I wasn't happy about the circumstances, but I didn't dislike you. Besides, that wasn't the first time we met." He smiled and the light intensified in his eyes. "The first time I met you was when you were wearing that polka-dot bikini on the beach."

She giggled and glanced away, embarrassed. "Not how I would have liked to have met you, if I'd been given a choice—either time."

"I have no complaints." He smiled. "The only thing better than that bikini was seeing you last night…in the moonlight. *Damn*." He exhaled. "I can't tell you what that did to my heart."

Speaking of hearts, hers sputtered in her chest. Part of her was questioning what they were doing and if it was the smartest thing, but the overwhelming majority of her didn't care. All she wanted was him and this moment.

He kissed her forehead as if it was a question. There was only one answer.

She moved to him, taking his lips with hers… owning him with her mouth as he had once owned her with his.

He took her face in his hands, his fingers gripping her and pulling her harder against his mouth like he was as hungry for her as she was for him.

She unzipped her coat and let it drop to the ground in a flurry of motions, all while refusing to break their heated kiss.

His tongue swept against hers, making her ache for more…for all of him. She needed to feel him inside her.

He let go of her hair and pulled her shirt over her head, followed swiftly by her sports bra.

I should have planned that better, she thought.

However, he didn't seem to mind as he kissed the hollow at the bottom of her throat and moved his way down. His hair smelled of sweat and fresh air and she pushed her face deeper into it as he popped her nipple into his mouth, forcing her to hold on to him out of fear the sensations would bring her to her knees.

He flicked his tongue against her as she closed her eyes, and he unzipped his pants and worked himself loose. He let go of her with his mouth and lifted her and moved her legs to wrap around his waist. He moved toward a birch, its papery white bark pressed against the middle of her back. He kissed her hard as he entered her.

She gasped with the beautiful ecstasy of feeling him inside. He was so big, and she stretched around him. He moved slowly at first, letting her body welcome him fully. She could feel her wetness on her thighs as he moved more quickly. Every thrust drove her closer and closer to the edge.

Hard enough to help, but soft enough not to hurt him, she bit the top of his shoulder. The action made him drive gloriously harder into her, faster, and she had to let go of him as she leaned her head back with a moan.

"Leo." She breathed his name, and it felt nearly as erotic coming off her tongue as he did inside her.

He paused, looking at her. He kissed her softly, slowing his stroke. She grabbed ahold of the tree and arched her back, working her body in rhythm with his until she could feel him grow harder—to the point of no return.

She didn't want to let him release, not yet.

"Leo," she said his name as if begging. "Lay down."

He wrapped her in his arms, moving deeper into

her as he moved them down to the ground. As they moved, he groaned, and she could tell that he was fighting his body.

If they had only these few stolen moments together, she wanted to ride them out.

The ground was covered with a mat of soft grasses and early summer flowers. She plucked a yellow and brown arrowleaf and, taking a moment so he could slow down, she pushed up his shirt and traced the flower down the line of muscles at the center of his chest.

She had known he was muscular, she had seen him rowing, but seeing him through his shirt and seeing his muscles exposed and awash with the colors of the sunset on his skin…there was no question in her mind that he was her Adonis.

She dropped the flower on the ground beside him and stared at the perfection of him and this moment. This was so much better than anything she had ever even imagined. With time, she couldn't even begin to dream about the heights of euphoria they could reach.

As she lowered herself down more, he was so large that it made her ache in a way she had not experienced before. Gentle at first, she moved on him. Driving her hips back and forth. She'd never been on top of a man. This was so new, so fresh. She was at the mercy of her body's wants and as she answered them, she felt her own edge nearing.

It was too soon, though. She had made him wait. Now she was the one who wanted to pause, but as she slowed he took hold of her hips. He moved her on him, keeping the pace she had been going.

"It's okay, baby, let it go. Don't fight it," he said softly, coaching her as he moved her on him. "I want to see you release. This is for you."

The words were enough to push her past any restraint she held and her body melted. Tilting her head back, as she moved to close her eyes she spotted the moon. With it, she howled.

Chapter Twenty-Three

He would live this morning a thousand times thanks to his memories. After running the bikini bottoms to the crime lab and making it back to his house and Chewy, they had made love three more times until they had both passed out in the morning, fully aware that their need for carnal lust would cost them in sleep—and neither of them had batted an eye.

When nature had finally called him from bed, he'd been forced to gently extract his numb arm from under her body. He had held her all night, afraid to give up a single moment of having her so close.

He pumped the blood back into his hand as he stood at the coffee maker and waited for it to brew. As he stood there, flashes of everything that had happened between them last night filtered through his mind, and even as exhausted as his body was, he felt himself wanting more.

Aspen was perfect in every way, from the curve of her hips to the round tip of her nose. She was incredibly sexy, and he was grateful she had given him the chance to finish what they had started. That was definitely what it was—the end.

He pulled two cups from his cupboard and looked out the window at Chewy. He was running around the yard and sniffing wildly in his search for a wayward squirrel. Chewy hated the damned things and he didn't blame him; nothing blew a person's cover when moving through the woods faster than one of those little bastards.

Chewy tore off in the opposite direction and out of sight. He turned away from the window and set about grabbing a loaf of bread and a carton of eggs. He didn't have much in the way of food in his house, but he would make it work.

There were the sounds of soft footsteps moving toward him and he started to smile. "You should be resting," he said, turning to face her.

Instead of finding Aspen standing in the doorway as he expected, there was a teenage girl. Blood dripped down her face and covered her white T-shirt. "Detective West?" She said his name, but her voice was faint.

"Who are you? Are you okay? How did you get in here?"

She opened her mouth to speak as she pointed toward the back door where he had just let Chewy out. "I…I'm sorry."

The girl dropped to the floor in a heap. He ran to her as the blood flowed freely from her head, but he wasn't sure if it was from a wound or from her hitting the hardwood floor. She lay on her side, the left side of her face on the ground, and her eyes were closed.

He put his fingers against her neck, finding a slow and sluggish pulse. "Aspen!" he yelled. "Call 911!"

"What?" Aspen sounded groggy.

"We need an ambulance! A girl broke in. She's hurt."

Aspen ran out of the bedroom, already dialing. She was talking to the dispatcher, telling them to run a trace for his address.

The girl's lip was split, and it looked as though her tooth was chipped. Her eye was bloodshot and her cheek was black and blue, the bruise so dark that it bordered on black. If he had to guess, she was between seventeen and twenty-three, but in the swollen state her face was in it was hard to tell for sure.

Under normal circumstances, the girl was likely pretty. Now, however, her dark brown hair was matted with blood and stuck out at weird angles around her head. She was wearing leggings and as he assessed her, he noticed that the backs of her arms were bruised and battered. Without seeing her legs or torso, he couldn't be 100 percent sure, but she looked as though she'd had the living daylights knocked out of her before dropping before him.

A few minutes later, the doorbell rang and he rushed to let in the two men with EMS. It only took five minutes for the first responder to arrive, but it felt like an hour. He hadn't moved from the girl's side even though she hadn't responded since going down.

Aspen was still on the phone with dispatch, but she hung up as the team went to work taking vitals.

"Do you know who this woman is, Detective West?" one of the EMS responders asked. He recognized the man from the office, but he didn't work patrol enough to know his or the other EMS worker's name though the guy knew his.

Leo shook his head. "No clue."

"Any idea what happened to her?" the other EMS worker asked. He pointed out toward the street that ran behind Leo's house. "Was she hit by a car?" The man put his hands on her belly, palpating the area like he was checking for any internal injuries.

"I didn't hear anything, and we didn't see a car that belonged to the girl outside. She literally just walked into my kitchen. She said my name and that she was sorry and passed out. There was nothing more," Leo said, trying to remain calm and collected. "If you look at her arms though, she does appear to have defensive injuries. However, without further assessment, I'd hate to say that with any degree of certainty."

The guy took her limp arm in his hand and moved it gently as he inspected the injury. "I don't know if anything is broken, but we will have the doctors give her a look."

Within what felt like seconds, they had her loaded on the gurney and they had started an IV to provide a fluid bolus. The young woman remained unconscious as they did their work and readied her for transport.

He followed them out the front door and to the waiting ambulance.

"We will admit her under Jane Doe until she wakes up and tells us her name or she is identified," the first EMS worker said. "I'll let the hospital staff know that they can share information with you. Were you going to press charges against this woman?"

The common practice in this kind of case was to wait until after the hospital care was over to arrest a person as then the county wouldn't be financially responsible for the perpetrator. However, in the case of especially heinous or egregious crimes, they would arrest them bedside. In this case, the girl had merely broken an entry—and apologized.

"I'll decide when and if she wakes up. For now, just write your report as normal," he ordered.

The EMS workers gave him a nod. He watched as they took off down the road and toward the hospital, red and blues flashing. Several of his neighbors were standing outside their houses, curious about the drama that had unfolded at his place. He was sure he would be getting calls from his HOA president and every nosy neighbor under the guise of checking to see if he was okay, as soon as he went inside.

His phone was buzzing on the counter as he walked back into the kitchen. Aspen was sitting on a bar stool, Chewy at her side—she must have let him back inside at some point. "Do you want me to start cleaning up the blood?" she asked, motioning toward the pool on the floor by the back door and entrance to the kitchen.

He waved her off. "No, you don't need to worry about it. Thanks, though."

"Did you know her?" she asked, getting up and walking over toward the coffee maker.

He shook his head.

"She was here to see you. Do a lot of people know where you live? I would think that kind of information would be something you'd want to keep under your hat. Unless…" She paused, looking over at the blood on the floor. "Are you sure you didn't have a relationship with her or something? Something you didn't want to tell them or me?"

"Hell no." He nearly choked. "I wouldn't hide an ex from you or anyone else. I know we haven't known each other long, but I'm not the kind of guy who is about to lie to or betray someone I care about."

"I didn't mean it like that," she said, trying to correct her misstep. "I just know how it can be…and she *knew you*."

He walked over to her, put his hand on her shoulder and gently rubbed circles with his thumb to help calm her. "I wish I could identify her, but the thing is that there are a lot of people in this community who know me. I'm recognizable. That doesn't mean I can even name them."

"I know how it all works—you're a public figure of sorts." She grew more relaxed under his touch, but not nearly as much as he'd like.

After such a great night, it sucked that this was what they were dealing with. He had to remind himself that their stolen moments were just that—*stolen*. Reality and the needs of their worlds had barged back into their lives in a big way.

Chewy got up and wandered over toward the blood, sniffing it.

"No, Chewy. Leave it," he ordered the dog.

He didn't want to deal with biohazard cleanup, but then he rarely got to do the things he wanted when he wanted…which was why he needed to hold on to the thoughts of last night all that much tighter.

Grabbing the roll of paper towels and kitchen cleaner spray, he walked to the pool of blood on the floor. Aspen moved to help him, but he waved her to a stop. "Just drink your coffee," he said, motioning toward her cup. "I've got this. You don't need to worry about it." He turned to the dog. "If it wasn't for this guy, I wouldn't want to do this, either."

"Chewy, come here," she called.

The dog pranced over to her and sat back down at her side. He looked up at her and there was a look of love in his eyes. He loved that his dog loved her, but it would only make it that much harder when Aspen had to leave.

He started to wipe up the blood.

It would have been nice if there was a way he could explain to Chewy not to get too attached, and that this wouldn't last long and things would be going back to just being the two of them.

As he looked at the blood on his hands, it felt like it could have as easily been his. His sticky life-blood could have spilled as a result of the death by the thousand cuts that came with relationships—or, in this case, a *situationship*.

Chapter Twenty-Four

After checking to make sure the Jane Doe had gotten to the hospital and was safely tucked away, and after calling his team to let them know what had happened, she and Leo made their way down to the river to resume their search. The CFS was running hot and, thanks to their delay in getting out this morning, they would have to wait until they got down to the water to assess what their options were. But Aspen was afraid they wouldn't be able to get out there on rafts today, or in the near future.

Which meant as soon as she told John and Kitty, they would likely be sending her home. Her situation with them was, at best, tenuous and this inability to perform the duties that she'd been hired to do would undoubtedly mean they would send her and Chad packing.

She couldn't say that she would blame them, but she would also do her damnedest to make the argument that they needed to keep her on to help with the search—especially given their new findings.

Facing them will be a losing battle.

She watched out the truck window as she and Leo pulled up to the boat launch. Luckily, they were the first ones there so she didn't have to see Chad or anyone else's face pucker that she had failed to come back to their hotel last night and was now rolling in with Leo this morning.

With everything that had happened though, they could go to hell.

She followed Chewy and Leo out of the truck and toward the raging river. What had been questionable was now impossible. The water was running fast and ripping at the bank and in a matter of hours since they had last been out here, turned from a dark blue to chocolate milk brown.

Picking up a large stick, she threw it out in the water and watched as it raced past them as they moved down the bank. They weren't moving slowly, which meant that even if they could get out on the water, the current was moving too fast and too hard for them to adequately or safely search.

She was definitely toast.

"I'd ask what you think," Leo said, his face pinched into a tight scowl, "but I bet you are thinking exactly what I am."

"That my ass is fired?"

His scowl deepened. "They can fire you all they want, but you are here as mutual support, which means that you are here with us, and at our invitation. While they can choose to no longer pay you, you can stay for the rest of your allotted time—time that's already been approved by the sheriff and SAR."

Though she was sure that he had meant his words to make her feel better, they also made her feel as though she had been stabbed in the gut. *They could stay the week*—that was all.

What had transpired between them last night hadn't changed the reality that they and their time together were finite. Though she was a realist and hadn't truly expected anything to come of their naked time, she'd be lying if she said she hadn't been hoping that he would at least make a feeble attempt at getting her to stay.

She tried to swallow back the pain. She was being unreasonable at best and a hypocrite at worst. She had been the one steering the ship of their relationship, and he was only doing as she had instructed.

Besides, she was here for Genie first—everything else needed to remain in second place.

"I appreciate the offer," she said. "I would like to stay until we find Genie, if possible."

He motioned toward the river. "Yeah, it's totally blown out. There's no way we are going to find her if she's in the soup now."

There was a creak and *whoosh*. On the opposite bank, a huge green pine listed and tipped. The creaking grew louder as the falling tree splashed into the water. Its roots were still attached to the sandy bank, but as the river swallowed the behemoth the sand crumbled from the roots and cascaded into the swirling water. The chocolate milk turned into near mud, flowing hard and pounding against the tree.

Danger didn't even sound like a powerful enough

word to describe how out of bounds the water was proving to be—hell, it was *deadly*.

She'd had such high hopes after finding the bikini bottom yesterday. Yet, now it felt as if that would be the closest they would ever come to finding the missing woman.

With the speed of the water, her remains could have been to the ocean by now.

Leo whistled for Chewy, who was sniffing around the base of a bush. "Come on, buddy."

The dog ran over and he clicked him onto a retractable leash.

Her phone pinged. *Chad.*

From his text, they were back at the boat launch. She would have to tell him the bad news—even though she was sure that he was smart enough to realize what was happening, or what wouldn't be happening.

The entire team was there when they walked back.

Cindy's face was tight, and she had her arms crossed over her chest.

"So," Leo said, not bothering with the niceties while they were dealing with the impotence that nature had wrought.

"So…" Cindy repeated. "How is the girl doing?"

"Still no ID and she's not awake," Leo said. "Sounds like she has a brain bleed, and they had to do a shunt to relieve the pressure. No one has called looking for her, yet."

"Are you okay?" Smash asked, giving him a glance. "She didn't hurt you, did she?"

He shook his head. "I don't think that was her intention."

Smash gave him a brief nod. "Well, damn. You guys had one hell of a day already."

"It's been one hell of a week."

"Did your team manage to pull any further information from the evidence you located last night? Or from the gun?" Chad asked, but thankfully there didn't seem to be any weirdness in his tone.

Cindy offered him a small smile.

Yep, they were definitely sleeping together. Aspen smiled.

She should have been bothered by the fact that Chad had been a hypocrite. He had seemed to be so enamored of her and then could so quickly move his attentions to another woman, but she was happy for him. He could be a jerk, but that didn't mean that he didn't deserve to be with someone who cared about him. Plus this would make it easier for all of them.

At least until they had to leave.

She sighed. Thinking about their situation didn't make her own any easier. Maybe they had come to the same understanding. Oddly, considering how awful Chad had been to them, she felt for his and Cindy's impending loss.

"I'm thinking that we work in pairs," Leo suggested, pulling up a map of the area on his phone. "Let's each take five-mile stretches. This way we can cover fifteen miles of riverbank. Let's check in every hour, assuming you don't find something before." He gave a feeble smile.

Cindy nodded in agreement. "Steve and Smash, you guys take this section. Chad and I will work the next five-mile point."

"We'll use the drone," Chad said, sounding excited.

Cindy nodded her approval. "Leo, you and Aspen take the last stretch. Sound good?"

She nodded. "I think we should all plan to meet again after we get done, and we can go over everything we have."

Leo nodded and he started to reach for her, but checked himself and instead played it off like he was readjusting Chewy's leash. It pulled at her to know that he was struggling in wanting her like she wanted him.

As they separated, she and Leo got into his truck and made their way ten miles downriver. The point where they were supposed to start their search wasn't far from an old logging road, but they had been driving for thirty minutes already and they were still a quarter of a mile from where they would need to begin. It made sense that it would be so remote, but it still surprised her how inaccessible everything seemed to be in this state.

As soon as a person stepped out of the little town of Big Sky, it was like they were taking a step back in time. She had thought they had been in the middle of nowhere when they had found Malice, but that location was nothing in comparison to where they would be going.

"If we don't find Genie," Leo said as they bumped down the rutty dirt road, "I don't want you to take it too hard. This isn't the kind of country that lends itself to finding victims. We actually had a known drowning five years ago. The daughter got caught up in the rapids and the dad moved to save her. She ended up making it out, but he didn't. They saw him go under, but he *never* came back up."

"Never?"

He shook his head. "Last year, a hiker found a skull not far from where we thought we might find him. We sent it for DNA, but it turned out that the skull was an antiquity and was Native American." He paused. "I guess what I'm saying is that people go missing and haven't been found on this stretch of river for hundreds of years. We are just repeating cycles that have existed long before and will exist long after us."

She nodded. "I will still feel like I failed."

"I feel like I fail every day. In my line of work, a lot of the time all I can hope for is to solve crimes—but even if I do, that doesn't mean I bring justice. In that, there is a huge division. It's up to the county attorney to prosecute. I see crimes that are so egregious and yet, they are swept under the rug—sometimes for leverage in other cases or charges, and sometimes I never find out why."

"You're not a failure," she said, reaching over and taking his hand with hers and giving it a squeeze.

"And neither are you. We are just always going to be moving against the current of the world."

She couldn't help wondering if they were also going to get as lost as the woman they were looking to find.

He pulled the truck to the side of the road, careful to leave room for another car to get by if one came by them on the one-lane road. So far, they hadn't seen another vehicle. This kind of isolation was something that she could get used to, if nothing else but to be a reprieve from the stresses of their lives.

Maybe that's what this place had been for Genie, too. They had been looking so hard for her, but the one thing she hadn't really considered was the fact that perhaps her disappearance wasn't unintentional—maybe Genie had been going through so much between the divorce, work and family, that she'd chosen this place to end things for herself. That would explain the presence of the gun—even if it had been in a strange location.

She moved to the back of the pickup and pulled out her backpack, followed by Leo and Chewy who readied for their search.

Aspen opened her bag then took three bottles of water from the twenty-four unit case. As she was about to drop them inside, she spotted a little black square of Gorilla Tape on the inside of the backpack, near the bottom, that she hadn't noticed before. She set the bottles on the truck's open tailgate and opened her bag wide.

Leo moved beside her, grabbing the bottles.

She pulled at the edge of the wayward tape. Its edges were firmly adhered to the canvas bag, and she had to work to get it free. Removing the tape, she flipped it over. She gasped as she looked at the AirTag. Someone had been tracking her.

"You put that in your bag?" he asked.

She shook her head.

"What?" he asked, taking the tape and offending item from her hand and looking down at it. "Isn't this a GPS tracker?"

"Yeah, but it's not mine."

"And it's not anyone else's from your team?"

She shook her head. "We don't track each other without their knowledge and permission."

Her thoughts moved to Chad and how he'd admitted he'd been in her bag, but she didn't think he would have done something like this. There was no reason for him to; he knew where she was and there was nothing work-related that she had ever hidden from him.

"The only people I can think who would want to track me is the Manos family. No one else but my team, them and your team knows I'm here or what I'm working on." She paused as a possibility came to mind. "No one from your team would do this, would they?"

"Hell no," he said, shaking his head vehemently. "We don't do that kind of crap. If we did, we'd find our butts in court in no time. Montana is a little behind the times, but it wouldn't be hard to sell it to an attorney and a judge that placing a GPS monitor would actually constitute stalking." He paused, tapping his chin. "Though, to prove stalking, it has to happen more than once. Also, we would have to prove that people were conducting themselves in way that is threatening."

She felt the color drain from her face. "Do you think someone wants me dead?"

"I don't think anything points in that direction. I think someone just wants to know where you are at all times." He rapped his fingers on the tailgate. "If I had to guess, I'd say Chad."

Some of the blood returned to her body. Though she didn't like the idea of someone tracking her, no one had tried to kill her—at least, not yet. The thought made her stomach clench. "Nah. He has his own thing going on with Cindy."

"What? No way," he said, sounding absolutely shocked.

"Haven't you seen them together?" She motioned in the direction from which they'd come. "I bet money that they spent last night together, too. Why else wouldn't they say something about me riding around with you and Chad having to work with Cindy? Forty-eight hours ago he would have been all over my ass about it."

Leo chuckled. "That's funny. I guess I'm glad he found something—or, rather *someone*—to do with his time."

"Oh, my God, you did not just say that," she said, with a laugh.

He sent her a smirk that almost made her forget about what was really happening. He reached over and put his arm around her and pulled her into him as he gave her a soft kiss to the head. "Looking at everything, I think we should throw the tracker in the river. Let it float for a ways. Whoever turns up out of formation downriver…well, we will have our answer." He picked up the device and pushed it onto the piece of tape.

She couldn't think of anyone else who would have had access to her bag.

"You've never left it in the back of your truck?"

She zipped up her backpack and put it on, snapping the straps around her waist and adjusting it so it sat well on her shoulders as he did the same with his. Her thoughts moved to her time here. There were definitely times, especially when they had been in and out of the warehouse and in meetings that her backpack had sat in the truck unattended. This was a small town, and she hadn't been concerned about the backpack being stolen or tampered with.

"Yeah, I did." She really had been a fool.

As they started to hike, her thoughts went to all the people she had encountered since being here. Her thoughts moved to the reporters. At home, there were some who would do anything to get the scoop on a juicy story. Then there was Scott. If he really did have anything to do with this, then it would have been to his benefit to follow their every move.

Whomever it was, there had to be something to gain—or something major to lose.

As they got down to the river, Chewy picked up a large branch that was floating on the edge of the water.

"Look, we even have an assistant," Leo said, taking the stick from the dog.

It had a few teeth marks in the wood, but it would be perfect for their task.

"Good boy," she said, giving Chewy a scratch behind the ear.

Leo dabbed the stick with the bottom of his shirt, drying it the best he could. Then he wrapped the tracker in the tape to keep it dry and wrapped a piece of tape around the stick. He held it up with the large swath of black tape at its center. "You want to do the honors?" he asked.

"It would be my pleasure." She took the stick from him. "You hold on to Chew."

He clipped the leash on the dog and snapped it onto a carbineer on his backpack. "He's not going anywhere. Launch it." He smiled.

She drew her arm as far back as she could and threw the stick and its offending cargo as hard as she could with a grunt. Every ounce of anger and fear she had been feeling seemed to leave her hand with it. A laugh escaped her lips as the stick hit the water with a splash. It was strange, but with its release she felt free.

Chapter Twenty-Five

After about a quarter of a mile, Leo couldn't see the stick any longer. It bothered him more than he wanted to let her know that someone would be tracking her— it wasn't a big step to someone wishing or doing her harm. His hackles raised at the thought. If anyone dared to touch her, he would crush them.

What little riverbanks had been exposed yesterday were now inundated by runoff, forcing them to move into the brushy undergrowth and making it harder than ever to see. The grasses were so high that they hid the downed trees and branches, which grabbed at their ankles and tripped them up. Though he had known things were going to be tougher due to the conditions, he hadn't thought about the added difficulties of the summer growth and hidden pitfalls. They would be lucky to make it five miles in these conditions, not to mention the fact that they would also have to work their way back.

"Had I known that this was how things were going to go, I would have brought our other drone from Minnesota," she said, sounding somewhat winded from the brutal push through the gripping branches and heavy undergrowth.

"We have a drone back at my office. When we come back, I'll bring it out," he said, trying not to sound as tired as he was already starting to feel.

Though they had been going for over ninety minutes, they had barely covered a mile of the river as they had to keep pushing out of the underbrush in order to check the water. At this speed, he wasn't sure whether or not they would make it to their waypoint and back to the pickup before dark.

"I'm sorry for underestimating you," Aspen said, pausing ahead of him and Chewy and turning back.

"What do you mean?" He stopped beside her and looked out at the river. The water was roiling, reminding him of how glad he was that they had decided not to risk going out in those conditions.

"I mean that this search is probably one of the toughest I've ever been involved with. I didn't understand how hard it would be. I mean… I understood that there would be a variety of conditions, but I didn't realize the changes in elevations and… this…" She motioned to the briars and underbrush that surrounded them. "I really thought we'd have more time on the water."

He smiled, vindicated that he had been right in his initial indignation and annoyance with her team inserting themselves into his search. "If it helps, I'm glad you decided to stick your nose in," he teased.

"Oh…" she said with a laugh. "Is that what you think I did—stick my nose in?"

"Absolutely, and you know you did. You out-of-staters come in and think you are so much smarter than us backwoods folk," he said, rolling his eyes in contempt.

The action made her laugh. "Did you seriously just roll your eyes at me? What are you…ten?"

He loved when she teased him. Very few did. She leaned over and gave him a playful kiss on the cheek. "You are a pretty great man. I know why most people would be intimidated by you, but when you do silly things like that I get to see the real you. The you few others get to witness." She paused, letting out a long breath. "I hope you find a woman who is worthy of you. You need someone so special."

Did that mean what he thought it did? Was that her way of gently saying that while she could tease and kiss him, that they were never going to last?

If she had wanted to hurt him, a knife straight to the chest would have been more humane.

Then again, he had known what he'd signed up for; he couldn't be upset.

"So do you," he said, trying to muster the strength to say what was right, instead of breaking down and telling her to stay here with him and never go back to her real life.

She moved to him and he took her in his arms. Their kiss was long and deep and filled with all the things he wanted to say to her, but knew he couldn't. She wasn't destined to be his, no matter how badly he wanted her to be.

He wished he could hold her like this forever. Their

place was this river, and it was the perfect metaphor for all that he felt. His feelings had started off clear and calm, but over the last few days they had torn through his barriers and flooded the banks of his heart.

Chewy whined and pulled at his leash like nature called. Not really looking or paying attention, he unclipped the dog's leash from his backpack.

He put his arm back around Aspen and pushed his nose into her hair, taking in her scent. She smelled of floral shampoo, fresh air, sweat and cottonwoods. Even her scent called to him. She nuzzled her face into his neck and her lips brushed against his throat. The softness of her lips on him made him moan and she giggled.

"Hmm?" he asked, lost in the feel of her kiss.

"That felt weird," she said, touching his throat with her fingertips.

"What?"

"Your moan on my mouth," she said with a suggestive smile.

It reminded him of last night's adventure in the trees. What he wouldn't give to have her legs wrapped around him now. He would relive that memory for many years to come.

She pulled from his embrace. "We better keep moving," she said, but there was a rosiness to her cheeks that made him wonder if she was fighting her body as much as he was fighting his.

She was right in moving forward, though. They had both learned the hard way what would happen if they fooled around on work time—and he had a feeling that he wasn't done paying for his misstep a few days ago.

He took a moment to collect himself and then moved slowly behind her. The riverbank was steep to his left, but the brush lightened up as they moved forward and gave way to an aspen stump.

There was a bend in the river, and it forced the water to move so fast and hard that it was difficult to hear anything over the rush of the rapids. Some of the bank had washed out, leaving it cliff-like. Ahead, according to the maps, it straightened out and slowed, and in another half mile or so the river itself dropped a few feet. In the late summer, it created a small waterfall but this time of the year it appeared as only a deep swirling mass of water and currents.

His heart raced as they watched the torrential movement of the river.

They were never going to find Genie. Not with this.

Aspen paused. "Do you see Chewy anywhere?" she asked.

He looked around, whistling for the dog, but Chewy wasn't anywhere to be seen. He called his name, but again the dog failed to respond.

"He must have gotten ahead of us. Maybe he can't hear us."

"The last time we let him lead, we found Malice," Aspen said, a spark of hope in her voice.

"Chewy!" he called again, picking up his pace.

There were the manic sounds of barking ahead of them. The sound was panicked.

"Chewy!" he yelled.

The barking changed pitch, becoming higher and more frenzied, almost bordering on pain. He sprinted in the direction of Chewy's sounds. They didn't stop, but every few barks there was silence and then the fervor of barking would increase.

The sounds terrified him. Aspen was behind him as he ran as fast as he could through the thickening underbrush as they entered another thick and heavy willowed area.

He cussed as he rushed through the tearing limbs, one wild rose catching him on the cheek and ripping at his flesh. He didn't care. The branches could have his flesh so long as he got to Chewy in time to help him.

Chewy was smart enough not to go in water. He'd eyed it warily as they had been hiking together. Something else had to be hurting or scaring him. Sometimes old-timers put traps out in the woods and near the water for beaver and different animals. If his dog had gotten caught, he'd find the trapper and do whatever had happened to his dog to the person.

"I'm coming, Chew!" he yelled.

The barking grew faster and more panicked, but he was close. So close.

"Chewy!" he called, trying to pinpoint the sounds of the pup's barks.

The dog yipped, the sound coming from his left… near the river.

He charged toward the bank, breaking through the thicket. The ground under his feet crumbled, and he grabbed at the bush near him that had been hiding the drop. The bush tore away from the soil as the world caved in below him, sending him down. Chewy's barks were the only sound he heard over the rush of the water and the echo of his shout of surprise.

The water sucked him down, the bush still in his hand, now untethered by the earth. He gasped as he fell into the frigid water and the muddy river filled his mouth. He sputtered, trying to remain calm as the world around him became flashes of light and dark, brown and sky.

A woman screamed.

Chewy howled, the sound coming from downriver.

Water. So much water.

This had to have been how Genie felt.

They would only find his backpack.

Chewy.

There was the flash of movement on the bank and he saw Chewy's wet head bobbing over the surface of the water, coming toward him.

"No," he ordered. "Go back. Get help!"

Chewy ignored him, moving toward him in the fast current.

"Go back!" he screamed. A wave crashed over his head, pushing him down and under the water.

Something grabbed and pulled at his feet, reminding him of all the movies he'd seen with the ghosts of the underworld pulling at the living and forcing them to enter the realm of the dead.

The world was nothing but mud. Darkness. Fear. The roaring of the water in his ears. He couldn't breathe.

He struggled to swim, throwing his arms out in

the direction he hoped was up. The currents turned him, flipping him over and spinning him like a tumbleweed as he tried to swim. His hand hit a rock.

His lungs burned. He needed air. He needed to breathe.

He tried to throw his feet down to launch himself off the rock his hand had hit, but it was already gone, making him unsure if down was really down.

It was all so disorienting.

The darkness in his mind started to creep in at the corners of his vision.

Air. He needed air.

Fight. I have to fight.

The darkness moved in. He was losing this battle—just as he was sure Genie had lost hers.

This was it. With a single misstep and the urge to save his dog, he belonged to the raging river and the unrelenting grip of death.

Chapter Twenty-Six

Aspen screamed as she watched Leo being swept downriver. Every nightmare, every terrible thing she had witnessed…nothing compared to the horror of this moment.

"Leo!" she screamed. "Leo!"

She ran as fast as she could, but the underbrush held her back and Leo grew smaller in the distance. He disappeared under the water as Chewy swam out toward him. He didn't resurface.

A scream of anguish pierced the air, sounding so primal and pain-ridden that she barely recognized it as her own.

Leo was gone.

Chewy was swimming in circles, but soon he was pulled downriver and around the bend and out of view.

Hot, stinging tears ran down her face as she struggled to move faster. The world felt like glue, sticking to her and holding her down while all she wanted to do was run and save them.

The tears moved faster as she struggled down the

bank, careful to stay back and away from the invisible crumbling undercuts.

He was good in the water. Leo could get out.

However, he was still wearing his backpack. Waterlogged, the thing had to add a hundred pounds or more, and that was to say nothing of its likelihood to get snagged on something.

She tried to breathe and remain in control of the fears and possibilities that were running rampant through her mind.

Leo would make it through this. He had to make it through this. She had finally found a man who she could be herself with, unreservedly. The world couldn't steal him from her now. He couldn't die. She couldn't live without him.

HER SCREAMS RANG in his ears as Leo's head broke above the surface of the water, and he pulled a sharp, welcome breath into his burning lungs. He could do this. He could make it. He had to think.

His body slammed against something hard, and the pressure of the water pulled him back under. He grabbed at what he'd hit, his fingers tearing at the bark of a downed tree. He tried to press his fingertips between the jigsaw texture, but the chunks of bark ripped away as the water rammed against him and pushed him deeper under the strainer.

He grasped wildly, hoping to find any handhold that he could use to self-rescue.

His hand touched something cold, slimy. He moved fast, taking hold of whatever it was in hopes it would hold him. The water crushed him, but he pulled himself downward and broke free of the current created by the log.

For a strange moment, the world stopped moving and the water stilled around him. It was eerie and he opened his eyes. The dirty water stung his eyes, but as he looked down at what had saved him, he saw a human arm. He nearly gasped as he let go of the rotting flesh. The body moved as he released it, and for a flash of a second, he recognized Genie's sunken eyes and lifeless face.

He slammed his eyes shut.

His backpack started to sink, pulling him downward in the pocket of still water. He struggled, trying to free himself from the straps, but failing. Reaching into his front pocket he pulled out the knife he always carried. He sawed at the polyester straps that tethered him.

The knife was sharp, but his lungs were bursting in his chest as they yearned for him to open his mouth and gasp for another freeing breath of air. This was taking too long. He was going to die. He was going to die right here next to the remains of the woman he'd been sent to find.

Maybe they'd find them together in some haunting poetic beauty. Rescuer and victim, one and the same.

They'd probably use this event as some lesson to tell kids to keep them away from the water and to rescuers in order to teach them the terrors that awaited. If they were like he'd been, they'd think themselves smarter and more capable. How painful this lesson was, this lesson of humility.

Nature would and *did* always win.

He reached into his bag and took out a loop of rope, trying to work as fast as he could. As he slipped free of his backpack, he grabbed hold of Genie's wrist and slipped the rope around her. He closed his knife and pushed it back into his pocket. Moving around her body, he felt a thick chain clamped tightly around her neck. He followed the chain back, finding it wrapped around a branch of the tree overhead.

This river never wanted to set her free.

Making sure he had hold of the rope tied to Genie, he pushed upward off the bottom of the river and emerged from the top of the rushing water, stealing a burning breath. He searched for the bank. He swam as hard as he could, moving with the water instead of fighting the currents and the weight of his bag.

He slipped toward the bank, the rope still in his hand.

Ahead of him downriver was John Manos. Chewy stood next to him, prancing and barking.

The man held out a long stick, the one covered in tape. "Grab it! Grab the stick!" John yelled.

Leo stuck out his hand, his head bobbing under the water as he moved for the stick. It struck his palm, and he took hold with all the strength he had left in his body. The water grabbed at him as the man pulled him free.

John grabbed him under the armpits as he got closer, and he pulled him up onto the bank. His feet

were still in the water as Chewy came bounding toward him, licking his face.

He was alive. Chewy was okay.

"Mr. Manos…" he said, taking in gasping breaths.
"Thank…thank you." He lifted his shaking hand and
gave the man the rope before the answers to so many
questions could slip away.

Chapter Twenty-Seven

It took a few hours for everyone from his team to arrive, including Steve, who was going to be their primary diver on the SAR team today as he'd had the most experience in swift water. Aspen had been an emotional wreck ever since she had caught up to him. From where he had gone in, to where he had been pulled out had been over two miles. For Genie, it had been more than twenty from the beach where she had gone missing.

As soon as he'd caught his breath and did a once over on the wet Chewy, he texted his fellow officers at the sheriff's office, making sure they brought everyone. Then he'd let the SAR team know, via text, what had happened, that he was safe, and he had believed he had located Genie's body.

His hands had finally stopped shaking after an hour of sitting on the bank. Gently following the rope, he, Chewy and John worked their way upriver to the point where the rope was perpendicular to them, indicating the body's location.

At first, John had continuously asked him if he

was okay and if he needed anything, but after Leo seemed nearly catatonic as he stared out at the water with the taut rope in his hands, John finally stopped asking and they waited in silence.

He had been careful not to say anything. He couldn't, not until Genie's remains were out of the water and she had been positively identified.

For all he knew, when he'd been under water his mind may have been playing tricks on him. He had been low on air, and the worst thing he could possibly imagine was to tell John that he'd located his daughter and that she was deceased, only to later learn it had been nothing more than some sick hypoxic mirage.

Everyone was quiet and little had been said besides the prerequisite hellos. Steve and his dive team were busy setting out their gear and readying for the dive. These weren't the conditions they typically dived in, but given the situation and the distance from shore, they had agreed to help in the recovery of the body.

Leo wasn't sure how he felt putting his team into the water in which he had just gotten himself out of, but at least they were better prepared and they would work under a strict set of parameters and with safety lines. No one would go into that water without a team helping them from shore and acting as spotters.

Kitty and Cindy were walking together from where everyone had parked their cars about a mile away. Chad had brought the drone and was getting it ready to capture the footage of the teams at work as well as the body recovery. He appreciated the help.

Aspen fidgeted, her hands balling into fists as she looked over at John. Finally, like she couldn't withstand it any longer she turned to him. "Why were you tracking me?"

Kitty walked up beside her husband. "I told him to do it," she said, sounding petulant. "And look how it turned out. If we hadn't been, your *boyfriend* wouldn't have been pulled from the water. If anything, both he and you owe us your thanks."

Leo nodded. "Tracking someone without their knowledge is, at best, questionable and, at worst, we could argue that what you were doing was a crime."

Kitty opened her mouth to argue, but John took her hand and gave it a sharp squeeze.

"Given the situation, and how it has all turned out, in this case…" Leo paused. "I do owe you my deepest gratitude."

"What did you find in that water?" John asked. "Are you finally going to tell me the truth…don't you think you owe me—"

"Us," Kitty said, correcting him.

"Yes, *us*," John continued, "an explanation? More, the truth?"

He pursed his lips. "As I've told you from the very beginning, we have to be careful in what we release due to legal reasons. I absolutely appreciate your action in helping me, John. Without you I'm not sure I'd be standing here right now."

"That's not an answer," Kitty countered.

Aspen shot her a look. "Kitty, please… All we are asking is that you be patient for a few more minutes."

Leo nodded, giving Chewy a scratch behind the ear. "What I can safely say is that I believe I found a body while I was submerged in the water." *A body he wouldn't have found without his pup.*

"You don't think we know that?" Kitty argued, pointing at the dive team. "Is it Genie?"

Leo held his hands in front of his body as he delivered the tragic news. "I'm sorry, but I think that there is a good possibility that it is."

Kitty dropped to her knees, a strange wail escaping her as sobs racked her body. Aspen kneeled and wrapped the woman in her arms, whispering to the heartbroken mother. He hoped she could bring her some comfort.

John stared at him, the color completely gone from his face.

"I'm not saying that it is. We will need one of you to provide a positive identification," Leo said, putting his hand on John's shoulder. "However, that can wait. What I would recommend, given the circumstances and the possible state of the body, is that you let us retrieve the decedent and let us move her to the crime lab where they will clean her up. I think it could be very hard to see her come out of the water. I don't want to put you through that."

John looked from the dive team to the water. Leo said nothing as Kitty's sobs filled the disquiet between them. After a long moment, John squatted beside his wife. "Baby, let's go back to the condo and let them do their work." He glanced up at Leo and gave him a grateful nod. "I'm sure they will call us as soon as they have any definitive information. Isn't that right?"

Leo nodded.

Kitty looked up, and there were tears pouring down her face. "Please...call us as soon as you can. Either way."

"I will let you know as soon as I can." He thought of Scott Gull. Legally, he'd be the first person he'd have to notify of the death.

Aspen helped Kitty to stand. Leo and Aspen watched together as the couple walked down the trail and headed back toward their car. When they slipped behind a far set of trees and disappeared into the forest, Aspen finally turned to Leo and threw her arms around him.

"I'm so glad you're okay," she said, but there was terror flecking her words. She reached down and patted Chewy's head. "What about you, you little stinker?"

"We're fine. Just a little shaken up." He gave her a kiss to the top of her head, no longer caring who saw them.

"Are you hurt at all?" she asked, leaning back and looking him over like they hadn't just spent the last few minutes together.

"I'll be fine, like I said. I just got rattled." He closed his eyes, and he could feel his body swirling out of control in the water again. He would never forget that feeling, and he was certain it was a sensation that would fill his nightmares for many nights to come.

That was to say nothing of the woman's face in the muddy water—she'd only been inches from him—and the feel of her skin slipping in his hands…

"You're not okay," Aspen said, hugging him tighter.

He couldn't tell her that she was right, but he wasn't in a place or position to let others see how badly he was struggling with the events of the day. Later, he would debrief and could sit down and process what had occurred, but for now he needed to get through this and the rest of the day.

"I can't tell you how much you mean to me," he said, whispering the words gently into her hair for only her to hear. "I needed your touch."

She pressed her head against his chest as though she was listening to his heart, and he found the action so sweet and pure. "Our hearts and our souls are in sync," she said, looking up at him with a gentle smile. "I'm not going anywhere…when you're ready to talk."

"I know that, Aspen, and I'm so grateful," he said, lifting her hand and giving it a sweet kiss. "Let's get through this."

"As long as we're together, everything will be okay," she said, meaning to reassure him but then also reminding him that this could be the end of their time together. If these were Genie's remains, she had no reason to stay.

It wasn't fair, but for a split second he wanted to

believe he'd been wrong about the face he'd preliminarily identified.

He squeezed her hand as they started to walk toward the divers. The future could wait.

Steve wore a wet suit and had a single tank, and was getting his mask wet and ready.

Smash was getting the throw bag ready in case he needed it, but was also readying a safety rope for Steve to hold. "You need to be careful out there," he said to him. "I want you to make sure you don't get wrapped up."

Steve gave him a thumbs-up as he waded into the water. "Four hard tugs mean I'm ready for you to start pulling."

Smash returned the gesture as Steve took to the water. There was a steep drop-off and Steve disappeared into the water. The rope moved as he watched.

Leo's stomach churned with anxiety for the man who was now searching the area where he had come so close to dying. Steve would be fine. He wasn't tumbling and he wasn't searching for air. Though the water was fast, he was wearing weights and prepared for the conditions.

Leo tried to remain calm. Thankfully, Aspen stepped to his side. Just her presence made him feel more at ease. It was odd how in very little time so many things had passed between them, so many feelings and shared moments—moments that had changed them and brought them closer together. In a matter of days, she had become his everything.

Everyone was silent as they stared at the water eddying behind the massive log in the water. When he'd first found himself pressed against it, he'd known it was large, but looking at it from above he now realized it had likely been one of the old-growth trees. It struck him how this behemoth had lived hundreds of years and had fallen victim to the fickle changes of the river and the pounding of its waves. Then, in its death, it had gripped Genie and had tried to steal him. It wasn't normal to anthropomorphize a tree, but what if this tree had a soul like a person. In its anger and rage, it had wanted to find comfort in death by not having to go it alone.

There were four tugs on the rope and Smash and the team started to pull. Steve appeared first, his mask poking out of the water.

In his arms was the discolored, muddy and battered remains of Genie. Her dark hair covered her face. As she came out of the water, he spotted the golden chain around her neck and there was a deep laceration where it had been holding her when he'd located her body.

He motioned for Chewy to lay down and stay put on the bank before he stepped forward to help. He and Smash grasped the woman under her arms and hips as they tried to gently move her to the bank without causing any further damage to the body. Her skin was slipping as they moved her onto the black body bag they had set out on the shore in preparation.

Aspen and the rest of the team helped Steve. He was fine, but he was quiet as he took off his mask and tank. There was a long moment of silence as they all gazed upon the woman. She deserved to be honored in this small way.

Looking out at the water, he silently thanked the river for letting them bring some comfort to the family and to their team by giving her up.

Her face and body were puffy, but there was no doubt it was Genie. She was consistent with having been in the water for a number of weeks. Her hair was swirled and matted in places, and dirt and flotsam caked her naked body.

She was bruised all over, and near her thigh there was a large gash where she had likely hit against rocks during her tumble down the river. For a moment, he wondered if under his still drying clothes he was even remotely as covered in bruises as her.

Hell, this could have been him.

Aspen turned away from the body for a moment, making him wonder if she had been thinking along the same lines. He moved toward her. "It's okay," he whispered, touching her gently on the arm.

She looked over at him, unspent tears in her eyes.

"I know," he said, not wanting to make things worse. "I'm okay. *We're* okay."

She touched his hand and gave him a nod as she tilted her chin to the sky and closed her eyes. It wasn't the time or the place, or he would have pulled her into his arms and just held her until she was ready to face this, but she knew as well as he did that they had a job to do. These were the moments when they weren't allowed to be human. They had to push through, but at least they were doing this as one and facing it as a team.

He stayed with Aspen, refusing to move until she finally took a long breath and looked to him, silently assuring him that she was all right.

"You ready?" he asked, making sure she wasn't going too fast.

She nodded.

The other members of his team were waiting for him, as was the coroner. "When you're ready, let's take a look."

The coroner squatted beside Genie's body and pulled back her hair. The right side of her face was bruised. He moved slightly and, taking out a pair of tweezers from his kit, he pulled at the skin.

The coroner looked up at him. "There appears to be perimortem trauma." The man paused, moving the tweezers around. "It's perfectly round, and I'd have to say that is consistent with a gunshot wound." He stepped to the other side of the woman's head, adjusted around her hair, and paused. "Yes, the margins here are shattered," he said, pointing toward the area in the hair. "Here is what looks like an exit wound."

This was no longer a drowning.

The man moved downward, examining the body. "Smash," he said, pointing at him, "can you roll her gently on her side?"

Smash squatted and pulled the body toward himself, exposing her back.

After a moment of poking and moving, he had Smash roll her in the other direction, then he finally looked up at Leo. "There's another area of trauma on her back." He motioned to her right side, just above the kidney area.

"Trauma?" Leo asked.

"Yes," the man said with a sigh as he started to move the bag around Genie. "I believe your victim was shot in the back." He started to zip the bag. "Her death was not an accident. I think we can assume that this was a homicide."

Chapter Twenty-Eight

John and Kitty had taken the news as poorly as Aspen had expected. While they'd known that their daughter was missing and that the body had likely been hers, it didn't make it any easier when she had called them yesterday. It had been a long night of documentation and writing reports, but she had never left Leo's side—even when they had gone together with the coroner to take the body to the crime lab.

It would take some time for the medical examiner to report their findings, but there was no longer a question as to the cause or manner of death—Genie was murdered.

Leo was in his office at the sheriff's department, on the phone. She was standing with Steve looking at pictures they had taken of the body when Leo finally opened his door and motioned for her to come back inside.

"Yes?" she asked, walking into the small office devoid of any windows or outside light. The effect of the flickering industrial lights overhead made her tense.

"I just got off the phone with the mother of the girl

who initially reported Genie missing. I didn't really pull any new information, but if need be I'm going to run down there and talk to her again in person. She said she had some photos she had taken on the beach that day, and maybe there was something else we could manage to pull." He ran his hand over the back of his neck. "She will be sending them my way."

"What about the video?" she asked. "You know, the one that Kitty used against Scott? Did you look it over?"

"Yeah, but just quickly. You want to watch it again with me?" He clicked on the video on his computer screen and it started to play.

Genie was screaming at the top of her lungs, calling Scott every name in the book. The video was out of focus, like Genie was holding her phone in her hand as they fought. The images flashed between black and moving faces and body parts.

There was the sound of a hard slap, but it was impossible to tell who had hit whom.

"You need to leave, Scott!" Genie yelled. "I don't want you. I've never wanted you." She called him a series of expletives, but her words were slurred.

"This is my house. I pay the bills. If anyone needs to leave it's you. You're high."

"I'm acting high?"

There was the sound of someone being punched in the gut, followed by a groan, but again she wasn't sure whose.

The video flashed to the beige carpet of the floor. There, she could make out a pair of women's purple running shoes and the tip of a cowboy boot. The feet moved, turning to the right as the video turned to the left and stopped.

Aspen huffed. "You're right. There really isn't anything, is there?"

He shook his head, running his hand over the back of his neck. "There was only enough to make it clear they were having a fight."

"And this was enough evidence for the other county to charge him with a PFMA?" she asked, somewhat surprised.

"They hadn't taken it to court yet, but yes. If a person feels at all threatened, they can call the police and it is enough for them to press charges. It would be up to the judge to decide further recourse, but there was enough here for a temporary restraining order to be placed against Scott."

"From what I saw, couldn't he have used this in his favor as well? To get a restraining order against her?"

"That would be tit for tat," he said, shrugging. "The result would be the same."

"Do you think it was her hitting him?" she asked.

He nodded. "It's definitely a possibility, but most people don't think of physical abuse happening from a woman toward a man."

"But it's not unusual?"

"A woman abusing a man? No." He sighed. "It is, however, uncommon for a man to call the police and report it."

"Do you think that may have been what was happening in that video? And maybe that was why Genie wasn't the one to turn it over to the police? Her mother was the driving force." Aspen stared at the play button on the computer screen like it would hold answers.

She couldn't wrap her head around what was going on.

"Even if Genie was the one who was abusive, it still doesn't explain how she ended up at the bottom of the river," he said. "But I think you might be onto something. Scott isn't the kind of guy who would open up and tell people his wife had been hitting him. I think it would be smart if we went to talk to him."

SCOTT ANSWERED THE door on the first knock, must having heard them pull up outside. "Hey, Detective," he said, shaking Leo's hand and then waving him inside.

Aspen led the way.

As Leo followed, he noted the beige carpet of the living room that perfectly matched the carpet in the video they had watched in his office. The place was clean enough, but not so clean to make him think Scott had scrubbed it down before they'd shown up. Scott was barefoot, but there was a pair of purple running shoes and brown cowboy boots perched beside the front door that matched those from the video.

"I appreciate you making yourself available for us on such short notice," Leo said.

"Yeah," Scott said, leading them toward the couch and motioning for them to take a seat. "I'm glad y'all found Genie. Thank you. And yeah, thanks for lettin' me know."

"Have you heard from her parents at all?" Leo asked, sitting down on the leather couch beside Aspen.

Scott shook his head. "I'm sure they think I got somethin' to do with it, but I'm tellin' y'all there's no way."

The guy was fidgeting as he sat down in his recliner. He was pinching the fabric of his jeans and twisting it in his fingers as he talked to them, clearly nervous.

"Scott, *did* you have anything to do with your wife's death?" Leo asked.

Scott threw his hands up in the air. "Absolutely not," he said, shaking his head. "I loved her. I did. She was the reason I came up here from 'bama."

From his body language and the tone of his voice, Leo wanted to believe him. Yet, some people had devious gifts when it came to the art of deceit.

"Did you and your wife ever have physical confrontations?" he asked.

Scott dropped his hands back down to his pants and started pinching the fabric again. "Yeah."

"Can you explain this video of you and Genie fighting?" Leo lifted up his phone and started to play the video he and Aspen had just watched at his office.

As it came to a stop, Scott sat in silence.

"Scott?" Aspen asked softly. "Did you slap your wife?"

"I tried to tell the cops who arrested me that she was the one who went to throwin' hands," he said, finally looking up.

"Did you hit her?" Leo asked, needing a clear answer.

"I'd be lyin' if I said I didn't get pissed off at her, but as mad as she made me… I never once touched her in anger." Scott looked him in the eyes. "I loved her, and my momma raised me a gentleman."

"What were you guys fighting about?" Aspen asked.

Scott shifted in his chair and his gaze moved to the hallway, but he didn't answer.

"Is there something you haven't been telling me, Scott?" Leo pressed. "If there is anything that is going to turn up on or in Genie's body that I need to know about, please tell me now. I don't want to have to come back here with information I learn after the fact that could potentially be damning for you or anyone else."

Scott wrung his hands.

"Scott, Kitty alluded to the fact that Genie had a drug problem," Leo said.

Scott jerked and shifted his gaze to them. "Why would she tell you?"

Aspen glanced over at him like she had heard the admission, too.

"So, you're not denying the fact that Genie was using drugs?" he asked, leading Scott to give him the answers that they all needed.

"Genie had gotten in a bad way," Scott said, looking torn. He stood up from his chair and started to pace around his small living room. He picked up a misplaced handmade quilt and started to fold it, like he needed something to do with his hands. "She and her best friend, Edith, were peddling meth. When

I found out…that was the fight. I kicked her out." Scott placed the blanket on the back of his chair and walked toward his television, which was sitting on an old, rusting trunk.

Leo took out his phone. Opening up social media, he typed in the woman's name. There, at the top of the list, was the individual who'd barged into his kitchen, bloody and battered. He tried to control his excitement.

"Is this the person Genie had been using and selling drugs with?" he asked, holding up his phone in hopes Scott would positively identify her.

Scott nodded.

"When did you last see Edith?" he asked, thinking about the blood that had been smeared over the floor in his house.

Scott cleared his throat. "Last time was the day I got in the fight with Genie. She ran out when Genie started to hit. I don't think she wanted to catch a stray fist."

Or she didn't want to go to court to act as a witness—or worse, as an inmate getting arraigned on drug charges.

"Scott, were you or are you involved in buying or selling drugs?"

"Are you kiddin' me?" Scott countered, slapping his hands down on the blanket. "Drugs are what caused all this. If I'd been good with 'em, she'd probably still be alive and sittin' right where you are now."

Leo stood up and brushed off the knees of his pants before standing. "Scott, I want you to know how much we appreciate your time and help in this matter. We will be in contact with you as soon as we know anything else."

Scott relaxed and gave him a slight dip of the chin. "I just wanna find out what happened to my girl… whoever did this needs to pay."

Leo shook his hand in appreciation. "If you think of anything else, don't be afraid to give me a call."

As soon as they were in Leo's truck, Aspen turned to him. "I believe him. I don't think he hurt her."

Leo nodded. "Me, either, but I think we may have just figured out someone who would."

They made their way to the hospital, where Edith was still a patient. She was still listed as Jane Doe, but as he walked up to the third floor and her room, he was met by Jamie. She was standing outside her daughter's room, leaning against the metal door frame.

When she saw him, her face fell. "Leo," Jamie said, her voice faltering. "I'm so sorry."

He tried to control all the feelings that welled within him as he was vacillating between anger at the situation and the secrets that Genie's family had tried to hide, and relief in the fact that they were finally making progress.

"Hi, Ms. Offerman," he said, but as he spoke she twitched like his using her formal name was a form of flagellation. "How did you find out about your daughter being here?"

"I have a friend here, it's a small town—you know." Jamie ran her hands over her face. "I tried to call Edith after you stopped by. I wanted to make sure that she was okay, but she didn't answer. No one knew anything about her and I panicked."

"Is she awake?" Aspen asked, moving to peer into the room.

"I don't want you going in there," Jamie said, trying to move between Aspen and the doorway.

Jamie reached back and moved to close the door, but before she did, Edith's voice pierced the air. "Come in."

Jamie turned toward her daughter. "You don't have to talk to these people. Don't tell them anything until we have a lawyer."

Leo pushed past Jamie and walked into Edith's room. "Hi, Edith, I'm glad to see you again," he said, walking over to her bedside and touching the waffled blanket over her toes.

Edith twitched slightly. "I'm sorry for barging into your house. I didn't know what else to do."

"How did you end up at my house, Edith? Do you remember?"

Edith started to cry, tears cascading down her bruised cheeks. "I followed you home... I'm so sorry."

Aspen walked over beside him and put her hand on his back. "Edith, no matter what happened, if you tell us the truth, we can help you move past it."

"I didn't mean to kill her." Edith choked out the words. "Everything just went wrong..." she said between sobs. "The guy we bought the drugs from... when he heard what happened..."

"You need to leave!" Jamie said, moving between

Leo and her daughter. She put her hands on his chest and started to push.

"Jamie," he said, trying to remain cool and collected with his friend during this difficult time. He put his hand on hers but stood his ground. "Jamie."

She looked up at him and she started to cry. "She's my baby girl. She didn't mean to hurt anyone."

He squeezed her hands. "Jamie, your daughter shot and killed her friend."

Jamie sank to her knees, reminding him of the moment he had told Kitty her daughter was dead. He was filled with anguish for both mothers.

Aspen squatted next to Jamie. "Your daughter screwed up. You and your family are going to have some hard days, but at least she is alive."

The words tore at him. Here his friend was struggling, but at the same time it was her daughter who had pulled the trigger.

"Edith, I'm going to need a full statement when you can," he said, turning back to her. "We will make sure that good things can come from this, not just bad. For now, recover and I want you to work on getting and staying clean."

Chapter Twenty-Nine

A month later, Edith was sitting in jail awaiting trial for Genie's murder. From what Aspen had been told, it sounded like she would get at least fifteen years in the women's prison in Billings. According to Edith's statements, she had been doing meth with Genie on the beach early in the morning. Things between them had gotten heated as Genie owed their dealer money. Genie had pointed the gun at her, but Edith had wrestled it away.

She had shot Genie in the back as she had tried to run into the water. She'd gone down, and Edith had panicked. Not wanting to have Genie turn her in to the police, she had shot her in the head. The dog had tried to jump in after her, but like Genie's body, had gotten swept up in the currents. After they'd disappeared, Edith had set up Genie's clothing to make it look as though she'd fallen in—in hopes her body would never be recovered—and tossed the gun into the water. When she showed up at Leo's house a couple weeks later, it was obvious she had been struggling after the attack and that drugs had clearly won.

Thankfully, she had admitted everything and it had nullified any fears about the broken chain of custody.

Neither Genie nor Edith was innocent. Life had taken them down a dark path. In the end, it had cost them both their lives in very different ways.

While her heart broke for all the people who had been affected, Aspen was relieved to have found the answers they had been searching for. At least…most of the answers she had been trying to find. There was still one major question that haunted her—what she and Leo were going to do.

Since she had gone back to Minnesota, things were *fine*. They had been doing the long-distance thing, calling and video chatting as much as their lives would allow, but it hadn't been the same as when she had been in Montana.

Everything about the state called to her. She loved the open mountain air and the remoteness of the riverbanks—and the birch trees.

Her cell phone rang; it was Leo. "Hello?"

"Hi, babe," he said, but there was something off in his voice.

"What's up?" she asked, excited at hearing from him but worried at the strain in his tone.

"I'm having a bit of a problem," he said.

Her heart sank. This was it. She was sure of it. They were breaking up. "What's going on? Are you okay?"

"Actually—" there was a long pause and there was a tap on her front door "—I am lost."

She stood up and walked out from her office. Standing on the other side of the glass was Leo. He was holding a handful of ropes, each piece tied in a shape that made it look like flower.

She dropped her phone and ran to the door, throwing it open. "Oh, my God, Leo!" Chewy was at his side, prancing as he waited for her to greet him. "And you brought my boy!" She squatted and gave the dog a quick pet before throwing her arms around Leo.

"Oh, you're crushing me," he teased, laughter marking his words.

"What are you doing here?" she exclaimed, not letting him go and pressing her face against the rope flowers and his chest.

"I got lost," he said, laughing.

She let go of him as she looked up at his face. "Lost? I don't think so, you are standing here."

He sent her a melting smile as he knelt down in front of her on her doorstep. "I just meant, I'm lost without you. I need you, Aspen. You are all I think about. You're the woman I want to be at my side for the rest of my life. Together we make each other better, and I never want to spend another moment apart."

She clasped her hands over her mouth as he reached down to Chewy's collar where he'd attached a little box. He opened it and retrieved a little velvet case.

"I know it's not a big diamond ring," he said, opening the box. Inside was a solid gold band inlaid with channel diamonds. "I can get you something else if you don't like this, but I wanted something that you could always wear—when we are working in the river or when we have our hands in the mud. I want you to know that I'm always with you. Aspen, will you marry me?"

She bounced from foot to foot as she nodded with excitement. "Yes, Leo… I'll marry you."

He moved to take the ring out of the box, but paused. "Wait, one more question…" He smiled.

She stopped moving. "What?"

"Will you also adopt Chewy as your dog? It's critical…make or break."

She giggled as she put her hand in his and helped him to stand. "If you think I'd want you if you didn't have a dog, you'd be ridiculous. I like him almost more than I love you," she teased, laughing as she pressed her lips against his.

"Never mind then, you can't marry me," he joked, moving the ring box away.

She grabbed his wrist. "I don't think so. I think the ring is perfect, and you already made your offer. No renegotiating," she said with a smile. "Yes, my Leo… I will adopt Chewy."

He reached into the box and took out the ring. "And, just to be clear, will you marry me?"

"You know I will. I've wanted to almost since the moment I met you."

He slipped the ring on her finger. "Any conditions?"

She nodded. "Two."

He pulled her into his arms, kissing her forehead as he held her. "And they are?"

"One, we have to get married at the top of a mountain after I move to Montana and join your search and rescue unit."

"Easy. Done." He ran his hand over her cheek and gazed into her eyes. "And what is the second?"

She smiled wildly and her heart threatened to burst in her chest. "You have to love me forever as I will love you."

"This is the easiest negotiation I've ever taken part in," he said, leaning down and kissing her lips. "I can promise you…you have my entire heart and it will be yours until the end of time."

* * * * *

Look for
Helicopter Rescue,
the first book in Danica Winters's
Big Sky Search and Rescue series,
available now wherever
Harlequin Intrigue books are sold!

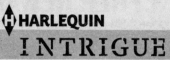